"Do you know what I'm wondering?"

Bernadette stirred uneasily in her sleeping bag as Sam continued. "You said when you have those feelings about a man that you pray until they pass. I'm wondering just how often that kind of prayer becomes necessary."

Bernadette felt guilty heat suffuse her. "Not often," she answered in a tight voice.

Sam's mouth tilted in derision. "And I always thought nuns didn't lie. Tell me, just out of curiosity . . . are you praying now?"

Bernadette closed her eyes. "As hard as I can," she said impulsively—and, as it happened, honestly.

'him tense. He stayed where
 otionless and silent except
 dy sound of his
 en he abruptly

LYNN TURNER is a going concern. In addition to keeping house for her husband and two sons, she teaches creative writing and works as a remedial reading instructor in Indianna. And on top of that she writes and still finds time to dabble with oil paints and sew occasionally. How does she do it? She says she has a button that reads: The only thing domestic about me is that I was born in this country. Oh well... Lynn's dubious attitude to housework is readily made up for by her storytelling talent.

Books by Lynn Turner

HARLEQUIN SUPERROMANCE
134—A LASTING GIFT
203—DOUBLE TROUBLE

HARLEQUIN TEMPTATION
  8—FOR NOW, FOR ALWAYS
 56—ANOTHER DAWN
 75—UP IN ARMS

These books may be

Don't mi

LYNN TURNER

forever

Harlequin Books

TORONTO • NEW YORK • LONDON
AMSTERDAM • PARIS • SYDNEY • HAMBURG
STOCKHOLM • ATHENS • TOKYO • MILAN

Harlequin Presents first edition June 1986
ISBN 0-373-10893-1

Original hardcover edition published in 1985
by Mills & Boon Limited

CHAPTER ONE

BERNADETTE CHAPMAN hesitated in the narrow doorway of the low, dimly lit room. Like many in the port of Mombasa, the building was very old, possibly even ancient. The only concessions to the twentieth century seemed to have been the worn and faded—and filthy— linoleum on the floor and the installation of electricity. Flyspecked bulbs emitting a sickly yellow light hung suspended above each of the half dozen rickety tables scattered around the room, and a sluggish ceiling fan stirred the dank, smoke-laden air.

The mingled odours of tobacco, soured sweat, the fumes of distilled spirits, and the distinct, sharp smell of ammonia didn't seem to bother her as she let her eyes adjust to the light, or the lack of it. She was too absorbed by her mission to be offended, and besides, she'd smelled worse.

Though to look at her, no one would have guessed as much. In her dark cotton skirt, neat white muslin blouse, and low-heeled shoes, she looked totally out of place, as if she'd got lost in the narrow maze of streets and wandered in by mistake, or perhaps to ask for directions. Small—barely five three and seven stone dripping wet—with large violet eyes in a pale heart-shaped face and a short, straight cap of sleek sable hair, she looked more like one of her students than an accredited teacher and librarian, which was what she was.

As might have been expected, her presence didn't go unnoticed for long. The beefy, dark-skinned bartender was the first to become aware of her. He put aside the towel in his hand with slow deliberation and approached her end of the scarred wooden bar.

'Help you, Miss?' he asked with a frown, his massive hands braced on the pock-marked wood as he leaned forward slightly.

5

Bernadette's head moved in a negative gesture. 'I don't think so, thank you.'

She sensed rather than saw his surprise at the calm response; her eyes were busy scanning the dozen or so occupants of the room. She'd been given a description of the man she was looking for, and she saw no need to ask if he was here. She was perfectly capable of determining that for herself. And anyway, she suspected the bartender was prepared to lie through his teeth if she asked him outright. Her chin came up a little as she spotted a likely looking head bent over a hand of cards at one of the tables and stretched for a better view of the man.

She heard the bartender mutter something as she started forward, but didn't turn to see if he was addressing her. One by one, heads began to swivel as she crossed the room. Faces—some ebony dark, others more the colour of cinnamon or chocolate, and one or two startlingly pale in comparison—turned in her direction, to stare as if she was some kind of space creature who'd suddenly materialised out of thin air. She felt the curious brush of their eyes, but neither looked at them nor faltered in her approach until she stood beside the man she'd picked out from the doorway. Oddly, he was the only one in the room who hadn't looked up; he didn't even seem aware of her existence, his concentration fixed on the cards in his hand while he rolled a long thin cheroot between his teeth.

'Colonel Forrester?' Bernadette enquired politely. 'Colonel Sam Forrester?'

The others shifted their attention from her to the man she'd addressed, their expressions watchful and guarded. He ignored her query, and almost a full minute passed in silence while he examined the cards in his hand. Then he casually laid them face down on the table in front of him and muttered, 'I'm out,' in a deep, gravelly voice around the cigar. And then, to Bernadette's utter astonishment, his chair scraped back from the table and he was on his feet, taking her left arm in a bruising grip. Before she could fully take in what was happening, she found herself back out on the street, being dragged along to an aperture between two buildings which she supposed must pass for an alley.

The thought crossed her mind that she might have approached the wrong man, and that if she had, she could well be in even worse trouble than when she'd set out from the hotel an hour ago, but she gave no sign of fear as he shoved her a few feet down the alleyway and then abruptly released her, placing himself between her and the street. Her right hand lifted to rub at her arm, where his fingers had dug into the flesh. She wasn't the type to frighten easily, and she'd learned during the past few months that any show of weakness was usually a mistake on this exotic, mysterious continent. She faced the big man calmly, her gaze clear and direct as she met his narrowed eyes.

'*Are* you Colonel Forrester?' she asked in the firm, no-nonsense tone she used in the classroom, and thought she saw his mouth twitch, though it was hard to be sure when he still had that noxious cigar clamped between his teeth.

'Who's asking?' he retorted as he folded lean brown arms across his chest.

He was wearing khaki trousers and a matching long-sleeved shirt, with the sleeves rolled to above his elbows and the buttons unfastened halfway to his waist, revealing that though he didn't have an excess of body hair, what he had was dark and coarse.

Bernadette released a resigned sigh; she had been warned, after all. 'My name is Bernadette Chapman, and I'm a teacher in a private school for girls near Bulawayo.'

'Bulawayo!' His surprise showed only in the way he repeated the word. Otherwise, he might have been carved from granite. 'You're a long way from home, aren't you, Miss Chapman?'

There was mockery in the drawled question, but Bernadette chose to ignore it. The question itself was merely rhetorical, and so she ignored it, too.

'Are you going to tell me whether or not you're Colonel Sam Forrester?' she asked with just a trace of impatience.

'I haven't decided,' was the lazy reply. 'Why don't you tell me why you're looking for him. Better yet, why you're looking for *anybody* down here.'

The mockery had become open derision as he subjected her to a hard stare, and Bernadette felt her temper rise in response.

'You think I'm a fool for going into that place alone, don't you?' she asked, her voice cool and controlled.

'Among other things, yes,' he confirmed.

'I had a good reason.'

'Tell me about it.'

'Not until *you* tell *me* whether you're the man I'm looking for.'

His face was partially in shadow, but she thought she detected a gleam in his hooded eyes as he reached up to remove the cheroot from his mouth. It had gone out, she noticed with amused satisfaction.

'Okay. I'm Sam Forrester. And you're even farther from home than I thought. New England, I'd say. Vermont?'

Bernadette blinked her surprise. 'No, Connecticut. But how on earth——'

'What do you want with me, and who sent you down here after me?' The questions rapped out without warning, catching her unprepared.

Her confusion only lasted an instant, though, and then she recognised his tactics. She gave a slow, disappointed shake of her head. 'That wasn't necessary colonel. I'm here because I've been told you can help me locate a man named Claude Dorleac. Can you?'

His eyes narrowed to slits, and instead of answering her question he threw another one back at her.

'Who told you that?'

'The bell captain at the hotel where I'm staying, Timothy something-or-other. *Can* you help me find this Claude Dorleac?'

'Timothy Ngulu.' He supplied the man's last name, though it meant absolutely nothing to Bernadette. He was eyeing her thoughtfully, his head tipped back a little as he idly rolled the cigar between thumb and forefinger. 'I might be able to track him down for you. Why do you want to contact Claude?'

Bernadette sighed again, this time in exasperation. 'Is it really necessary for you to know that?'

'Only if you want my help,' he replied flatly.

She didn't answer for a minute. She wished the sun wasn't at his back so she could see his face clearly. She was good at reading people's expressions, especially what was in their eyes, but so far she hadn't even had a good look at his—didn't even know what colour they were. Something told her it probably wouldn't have helped, though. This man wouldn't give anything away, not by look nor word nor gesture, that he didn't intend to give away.

'It's a long story,' she said finally. 'I'm here with the headmistress of the school where I work and several of our students. We had intended to be in Nairobi by now, but Mrs Althoff—she's the headmistress—has had a recurrence of malaria, and I think it would be best to take her straight back to Zimbabwe as soon as possible.' She hesitated again, choosing her next words with care. 'Also, two of the girls with us are the daughters of . . . an official, whose region is in a state of . . . upheaval, at the moment. Their father contacted us last night and asked that we return the girls to the safety of their school at once.'

'Hold it,' Forrester interrupted before she could say anything more. 'If you're talking about the region I think you're talking about, they're not having an *upheaval*, lady, they're having a damned civil war, which I suspect you bloody well know. These girls wouldn't happen to be the daughters of Prince Tzongari, would they?'

Bernadette did her best to hide her dismayed surprise. 'Yes,' she admitted with reluctance. 'His two youngest children. Since you know the situation, you must also realise why it's imperative that we get them back to the school, where they can be protected.'

'You have armed guards at this private girls' school, have you?' Forrester mocked.

'No, but we do have a twelve-foot stone wall

surrounding the grounds and a local chief of police who can be trusted implicitly. Also, the fact that the girls are students there isn't generally known. We'd like to keep it that way,' she added pointedly.

Forrester nodded. 'If you took a commercial flight home, you'd have to reveal their identities, and the information might find its way to some of their father's enemies.'

'Exactly. Your friend Timothy tells me this Monsieur Dorleac will fly anyone anywhere, at short notice, for a price. He also claims that you're the one person in Mombasa who can be counted on to know his whereabouts and how to contact him. So ... can you put me in touch with him?'

Her hopes were dashed by his succinct: 'No.' She closed her eyes briefly as a wave of bitter disappointment washed over her, then squared her slim shoulders and lifted her head with a poignant, graceful dignity.

'I see. You might have told me that before wringing all the details out of me, Colonel, but I suppose you must have had your reasons. I guess I'll just have to find another way to get the girls and Mrs Althoff home, then. My apologies for wasting your time.'

She started past him, but his hand came out to stop her, his fingers closing around her arm again, their grip measurably less cruel this time.

'Just a minute, Miss Chapman. I said I couldn't put you in touch with Claude, I didn't say I don't know where he is. At the moment he's delivering a load of ... cargo, to Kinshasa.'

'Kinshasa!' This time Bernadette was helpless to conceal her dismay as her eyes lifted to his face. 'But that's on the other side of Africa, over fifteen hundred miles away!'

'Very good, Miss Chapman,' Forrester drawled. 'I take it you teach geography in this school of yours?'

When she failed to respond to the taunt, he released her to stick the cheroot back in his mouth. His shrewdly assessing eyes raked her delicate face and slight frame, and then he seemed to lose interest as he gave a careless shrug and turned away to relight the cigar.

'Claude will be in touch with me tonight or early tomorrow. When I hear from him I'll pass on your message and find out if he's available. Wait at your hotel. I'll get word to you.'

Realising she had been dismissed, Bernadette nodded and walked on past him to the street. She was tempted to look back when she reached it, to offer words of appreciation, but she didn't. He'd made it clear that their conversation had been terminated.

He was an unusual man, a kind of man new to her experience; though in all honesty she could hardly consider herself an expert on men. From what little Timothy had told her, she had expected the mysterious Colonel Forrester to be cautious, distrustful and wary, and so she hadn't been surprised by his questions and had answered them willingly. He was a hard man, or perhaps it would be more accurate—and fair—to say a hardened man. He wouldn't be swayed by impassioned pleas of feminine hysterics, Timothy had warned. Just give him the facts, and he'll calculate whether to help you or send you on your way. And once he's made up his mind, he won't change it—if he promises to help, you can stake your life that he'll do everything he can.

Altogether a very unusual man, she decided as she entered the street leading back to the hotel. He even had unusual eyes. She'd discovered in those few moments when he detained her that they were grey, cool and calculating, and unblinking in their directness. She'd read somewhere once that gunfighters had eyes like that, and jet fighter pilots. She could easily imagine Colonel Sam Forrester in either of those occupations. She knew a moment's regret that he wasn't the man she'd be entrusting with their safety and their lives. He might be hard and callous, possibly even cruel at times, but she instinctively felt that once he committed himself to a job, he'd see it through no matter what.

She was so absorbed in thought that she failed to notice the tall, leanly muscled man in the khaki shirt and trousers who trailed her through the streets of Mombasa. He even followed her into the hotel, but instead of taking the elevator up, went straight to a door at the rear of the lobby and pushed through it like a man who knew exactly where he was going.

For the rest of the day Bernadette was kept busy supervising her young charges. Poor Mrs Althoff was so weak it was all she could do to get to the bathroom without assistance. The news that they might be going home soon had done a lot to lift her spirits, though, and Bernadette could only pray she hadn't raised false hopes in mentioning Monsieur Dorleac. She had judiciously *not* mentioned any of the manoeuvring which had been necessary to make the tentative, indirect contact with him. Mrs Althoff was as kindhearted as they came, but extremely conservative. She'd have been scandalised to know what sort of people her quiet, reserved Miss Chapman had been dealing with, not to mention where she'd had to go to do the dealing.

Keeping six high-spirited girls occupied without exposing them to the worldly influences of a city like Mombasa was a full-time job in itself, Bernadette decided wryly as she saw the last of them tucked into bed that night. They had never intended to stop here at all, planning to take the train from Moshi to Tanzania through to Nairobi for a few days holiday there before flying back to Salisbury. Mrs Althoff liked to combine school holidays with field trips, so that no opportunity was lost to educate the students and enrich their lives. They had all enjoyed the trip to view Mt Kilimanjaro, and were looking forward to an excursion to one of Kenya's game reserves before returning home. But Mrs Althoff's sudden bout of malaria had necessitated an abrupt change in plans, and was the reason they were all more or less holed up in three hotel rooms in the seaport of Mombasa instead of playing tourist in the more acceptable—to Mrs Althoff's mind—Nairobi.

Fortunately they'd been able to obtain a suite, so at least they weren't too cramped. Extra beds had been moved into two of the rooms so the third could be used as a sitting room during the day. Bernadette had dictated the sleeping arrangements with typical practicality. She and Melissande, who was twelve, bunked with Prince Tzongari's daughters Kaisi and Amira, seven and eight. Fourteen-year-old Patrice—the oldest of the students along on this trip—shared a room with Mrs Althoff and the two nine-year-olds, Lizbeth and Tumara.

'They're all finally asleep,' she whispered as she dropped into a chair beside Mrs Althoff's bed. 'How are you feeling? Can I get you anything?'

The older woman smiled and reached out to pat her hand. 'No, dear, bless you. I'm quite comfortable, just disgustingly weak. Why don't you get to bed, yourself? You must be exhausted.'

'I will, in a bit,' Bernadette answered as she rose to her feet. 'I'm feeling a little restless. I think before I turn in I'll go out for some fresh air.'

Mrs Althoff clearly didn't think much of that idea. 'I'm not sure that would be wise, Bernadette. This isn't Bulawayo, or even Salisbury. The streets are probably full of——'

'It's all right,' Bernadette cut in, gently but firmly. 'I won't go far, I promise. There's a café just outside the hotel. I think it's open all night, and you can get to it through a side entrance. I'll just go down for a cup of coffee and then come straight back up.'

She didn't loiter, knowing Mrs Althoff would try to persuade her not to go. It wasn't a matter of being stubborn or wilful, she just needed to be out of doors for a while. She always felt cooped up if she was enclosed by walls and a roof for any length of time, and tonight the feeling was worse because the girls had become bored and querulous that afternoon and it had taken all her ingenuity to keep them entertained. She needed some time to herself, a little peace and solitude in the open air, and then she knew she would feel recharged and better able to cope in the morning.

She folded a couple of travellers' cheques and put them in the pocket of her skirt along with the room key, then silently let herself out and locked the door behind her. Bernadette was no fool; she might not be intimidated by the idea of going out alone at this time of night for a cup of coffee, but at the same time there

was no use tempting the devil, as her grandmother
would have said. And an unescorted woman carrying a
bulging handbag would be a temptation few devils
could resist.

The café was nearly deserted. She supposed it was too
late for those who retired early, and too early for the
serious carousers. She took a seat at a minuscule table
for two near the hotel wall, and on second thought
ordered grapefruit juice, thinking the coffee would
probably keep her awake.

It arrived, she paid for it with one of the traveller's
cheques, and had taken a couple of tentative sips when
she became aware of the pungent odour of cigar smoke.
Mildly curious, she turned her head to the right, away
from the hotel entrance. A dull red glow pinpointed the
man's position, and she wondered why he was standing
on his own like that, beyond the light, instead of seated
at one of the vacant tables. Before she could look away
he came towards her, and she thought she understood
why.

'Miss Chapman.'

Even before he spoke she had identified him, by the
light, silent, smoothly efficient way he moved and the
aroma of his cheroot, which she belatedly recognised
the instant before he emerged into the light.

'Colonel Forrester, good evening. I've been thinking
about you.'

It was true. While her thoughts had been occupied
with other things for most of the day, he had been there
all the time, lurking at the edge of her consciousness.

'How flattering,' he drawled with lazy mockery as he
gazed down at her. 'I've been thinking about you, too.
May I join you?'

She would remember that voice as long as she lived,
Bernadette thought. It was low and slightly harsh, as if
he was hoarse from yelling at the top of his lungs all
day. Yet there was a deep resonance to it, as well. It
seemed to come from the soles of his feet, rumbling up
through that long, tough-looking body and somehow
being muted by the time it reached his throat. No, she
revised the whimsical reflection; not muted, but tamed a

little, civilised for the benefit of those who might hear it. The thought brought a quiet smile to her lips as she indicated the chair across from her.

'Please.'

As he slid into the chair she noticed that he'd changed clothes. He was wearing navy slacks and a snug fitting V-necked pullover of charcoal grey. The clothes had no doubt been chosen for their ability to let him disappear into his surroundings at night, and he did. If not for the cigar, she'd never have known he was there. She wondered what kind of man would want to make himself invisible, then decided she probably didn't want to know.

Seconds after he was seated a waiter appeared, polite to the point of obsequiousness as he asked what Colonel Forrester desired. Bernadette couldn't prevent a slight smile; *she* had occupied the table for a good five minutes before one of the waiters finally noticed her.

'Scotch and water, David, please,' Forrester growled, and as the young man hustled away he looked around and caught Bernadette's smile.

'You seem to be well known by everyone in Mombasa,' she said in explanation, and one corner of his mouth quirked upward.

'Known or known of,' he admitted drily. 'Which is sometimes more a curse than a blessing.'

His drink arrived in less than a minute, and this time he joined her in acknowledging the humour of the situation by allowing his hard mouth to soften briefly.

'You've heard from Monsieur Dorleac?' Bernadette asked when the waiter had discreetly made himself scarce.

'About an hour ago,' he confirmed. 'He can fly you out tomorrow morning, provided you're willing to share the ride and don't mind making a slight detour. He can still have you home by tomorrow night.'

Bernadette considered the conditions a moment, then agreed. 'All right. What time will we be leaving?'

Forrester raised his drink to his lips. There was a glint of malicious humour in his eyes as they met hers over the glass and he told her: 'Dawn.'

'Fine,' Bernadette replied without missing a beat. 'From where?'

'A private airstrip.' He set the glass down to fish a folded piece of paper out of his hip pocket. 'Here. Directions how to get there. If I were you, I'd arrange for a taxi with the night manager. You might not be able to get one when you're ready to leave, and Claude won't wait for you.'

'We'll need two. Taxis, that is. Thank you,' as she accepted the folded paper. 'Well, if I'm going to have everything ready by dawn, I'd better get back upstairs.'

He stubbed the cheroot out in an ashtray and rose with her, dropping a bill on to the table as he came around it, then accompanied her to the front desk and personally arranged for two taxis to be waiting at four-thirty in the morning. Bernadette asked about breakfast, and was told the kitchen wouldn't be open but that rolls and coffee could be provided. That would just have to do, she supposed.

Forrester stuck to her side as she crossed to the elevator, and at her questioning look remarked: 'You shouldn't be wandering around on your own. I'll see you up.'

She'd never have taken him for the chivalrous type, but she didn't protest that she wasn't in need of protecting, a fact she was to regret in the days to come.

Outside the suite she turned towards him, the key in her hand. 'You've been very helpful, Colonel.'

Once more she glimpsed that brief sideways quirk of his mouth, as if he was secretly amused by something.

'You may not think so this time tomorrow. Claude's services come high, and you won't exactly be travelling in luxury.'

Bernadette's slight gesture was dismissive. 'Money isn't a problem—we're fortunate in that the school has several generous patrons. And a few hours of discomfort won't seem like so much once we're safely home again. I can't tell you how much I appreciate your help, Colonel. A simple "thank you" hardly seems adequate.'

He slid one long brown hand into the pocket of his slacks and bestowed a lazy, narrow-eyed smile on her.

'Then why don't we see if we can come up with something a bit more substantial in the way of compensation,' he drawled, his deep voice laced with mockery.

Of course! Bernadette felt incredibly stupid. He probably expected some kind of fee or commission or something, for acting as go-between. How foolish of her not to have thought of it before! But her purse and all the money but one traveller's cheque were inside the suite, on a table in the sitting room.

'Of course, Colonel,' she murmured in embarrassment. 'If you wouldn't mind coming inside for a moment . . .'

And so saying, she turned to fit the room key into the lock, and missed the cynical satisfaction which pulled his hard mouth into a thin smile.

'We'll have to be quiet,' she whispered as he followed her into the room and she switched on a small table lamp. 'Mrs Althoff and the girls are sleeping next door.'

'No problem, honey,' came the harsh-soft answer at her back, and then there was a quiet click as the door was eased shut.

Bernadette picked up her purse and was in the process of extracting her wallet as she turned to face him.

'What is your usual fee for this sort of thing?' she asked absently. She was thinking that if he had it in mind to rook her, she was at his mercy; she had absolutely no idea what the going rate for part-time travel agents was in this part of the world.

Forrester frowned, looking puzzled for a moment before the frown cleared and his mouth twisted in a derisive smile.

'Well, that's certainly a switch,' he muttered under his breath.

'I beg your pardon?' Bernadette was doing some fast mental arithmetic, trying to calculate what she thought would be a fair amount.

'I'm flattered, Miss Chapman,' he drawled. 'But shouldn't you wait to see if my performance is deserving of payment?'

Bernadette looked up in confusion. What was he talking about? And then he confounded her even more by taking the purse from her hands and tossing it on to the sofa cushions.

'You're all the incentive I need, sweetheart,' he murmured as his fingers curled around her arms, and the next thing she knew, he was kissing her.

And she had thought he was unusual! Different! Bernadette didn't know whether she was more angry at him for assuming she'd be willing to show her appreciation in the time-honoured way, or at herself, for being so unbelievably gullible. One thing she did know, and that was that if Mrs Althoff should happen to wake up and wander into the room, her plans for getting them back to Zimbabwe would go up in smoke.

'Colonel Forrester!' she hissed as she managed to wrench her mouth free. 'Just what do you think you're doing!'

His husky chuckle came as a surprise, but it was nothing compared to the astonishment she felt when his arms slipped around her and he pulled her hard against him, his hands on her hips fitting her pelvis intimately—and perfectly—to his.

'That's good,' he observed drily. 'Perfect. Just the right amount of shocked virginal outrage. It goes with your looks—cool, innocent, and always in control.' His hands pressed her even closer as his mouth sought out the tender curve of her neck.

'Altogether, Miss Chapman, you make for one hell of a challenge,' he murmured against her skin. 'A man just has to find out what's hidden under that prim, prissy exterior.'

'Believe me, Colonel Forrester, you'd find the real me a big disappointment,' Bernadette gritted. Her neck was arched at an unnatural angle as she tried to evade him. It was an exercise in futility; the man had more arms than an octopus, and his firm, warm lips followed her every move, until she was ready to scream with frustration.

'I'll be the judge of that,' he growled in her ear.

Bernadette opened her mouth to contradict him,

which proved to be a mistake. His lips fastened on hers with a strength and determination she found unnerving, to say the least, and then she experienced the shocking invasion of his thrusting tongue as it searched and explored aggressively.

She was both appalled and outraged. How *dare* he kiss her like that! The man was depraved, totally depraved!

'Stop it!' she ordered breathlessly when he gave her the chance by shifting his head a little to one side.

'Come off it, sweetheart, you know you love it,' he muttered against her lips, and then his were locked on them again, his kiss even more abandoned than before.

Love it! Oh, honestly, the conceit of the man was unbelievable! Her eyes were wide open and glaring at him, but unfortunately his were tightly closed, his brows drawn together by the intensity of the effort he was expending, and the glare was wasted.

Fed up, insulted, and thoroughly disgusted, Bernadette did what she should have done when he first laid hands on her. The sturdy heel of her right shoe came down solidly on his instep, and when he muttered a surprised oath she bit down hard on his slack lower lip.

'Damnation! You little bitch!' he swore as he released her. He raised a hand to his mouth. His fingers came away bloody, and he stared at them in angry amazement.

'What the hell kind of game are you playing?' he demanded, but he didn't try to recapture her as she put a respectable distance between them.

'*Game!*' Bernadette's tone should have chilled him to the bone. She took a deep breath, striving mightily for control. 'I'm going to give you the benefit of the doubt, and assume your crude behaviour stems from the fact that you just aren't used to associating with decent women. Now,' as she marched to the door and yanked it open, standing aside to hold it for him, 'I suggest you leave, Colonel. On second thought, I've decided a simple "thank you" is more than adequate.'

He stared at her for a moment, his narrowed eyes

inscrutable, and then he inclined his head in a mocking little salute and strode past her without a word.

Bernadette closed the door behind him and locked it, then rested her forehead against the cool wood. She felt tense and angry and uncharacteristically rattled, and she was relieved beyond words that she had seen the last of Colonel Sam Forrester.

CHAPTER TWO

THANKFULLY, the girls were still half asleep and didn't complain about being dragged out of the hotel and bustled into the waiting taxis at such an indecent hour. Bernadette rode in the front car—a dilapidated jalopy that wheezed and coughed and backfired its way through the predawn city with all the vigour of a tranquilised snail—in order to direct its driver to the airfield.

The route they took was so circuitous that she wondered briefly if it had been Colonel Forrester's intention to lose them in the wilds of Africa. But then, finally, at the end of a twisting road that could never have been intended for motorised transport, the weak beams of the taxi's headlights swept across the hulking shape of an old tri-motor aircraft, and she breathed a sigh of relief.

The relief was short-lived as she stepped out of the taxi and got her first good look at the plane which was to take them roughly twelve hundred miles, over mountains and dense forests and unpopulated areas which were all but inaccessible to man. Oh Lord, what had she got them into? she wondered in dismay.

'Her skin may be a little wrinkled, but her heart is that of a young lioness in her first season.'

The voice was young and brash, and attractively accented. French, Bernadette thought, and then: Claude Dorleac, their pilot. A second later his slight, wiry body followed his voice out of the shadows beside the plane.

'Mademoiselle Chapman?' At her nod, he introduced himself with a gallant little bow. 'Claude Henri François Dorleac, at your service.' He jerked his head towards the plane with a boyish grin. 'Do not be deceived, Mademoiselle. Her engines are the very best that McDonnell Douglas makes, each with less than seventy thousand accumulated miles. She will deliver you and your *jeune filles* home safely, you have my word. Now, shall we get your luggage and the little ones aboard?'

Bernadette followed his lead, but she still had her doubts. Monsieur Dorleac looked like he couldn't have anywhere near seventy thousand accumulated miles, himself. If he was a day over thirty she would be very much surprised; twenty-six or -seven would be more like it.

As he assisted Mrs Althoff aboard he was considerate and respectful, but when it came Bernadette's turn, a sly wink accompanied his boost up. She was glad she'd worn jeans as he grinned up at her, hands on hips and his flight cap tipped back at a jaunty angle. He was probably a typical Frenchman, she decided: devil-may-care with the ladies, but completely serious when it came to business. And considering the business he was in, she supposed he was entitled to a little harmless flirtation now and then to relieve the stress.

Glancing around the cargo hold, where passengers took second place to freight and had to sit on benches bolted to the sides of the fuselage, she assured herself that the girls and Mrs Althoff were settled, then turned her attention back to M. Dorleac.

'Will we be taking off soon?'

He nodded once. 'On schedule, at dawn.'

'But I understood you'd be carrying another passenger.'

This time the young pilot's nod was accompanied by a crooked grin. '*Oui.* He will be here, Mademoiselle, never fear. He likes to cut it close, as you Americans say, but he knows I would not delay my takeoff even for him.'

Inferring from the remark that the passenger must be someone important, Bernadette started to turn away, intending to find herself a place on one of the metal benches. The sound of an approaching vehicle halted her, and plain old curiosity kept her in the door. As both she and the pilot watched, a Land Cruiser came hurtling towards them through the pale grey light, bouncing down the rutted road as if an advancing army was just around the last bend.

When the vehicle screeched to a halt three feet from
the port engine, Bernadette released her held breath in a
rush. She watched as the driver climbed out and loped
over to Claude Dorleac and they embraced, happily
pounding each other on the back. The newcomer was a
Black man, but that was all she could be sure of at that
distance and in the poor light. Then he stepped back,
looked up, and spotted her.

'Miss Chapman!' he called a cheerful greeting. 'I see
you made it all right.'

'Yes, Timothy,' she responded after a second's
surprised silence. What business the bell captain of the
Excelsior Hotel might have with M. Dorleac, she
couldn't begin to guess. Nor did she care to try.

'Will you be flying with us?' she asked politely.

His wide grin was a flash of white in the gloom, but
before he could speak someone else answered for him.

'Sorry to disappoint you, Bernie, but *I'm* the other
passenger.'

Oh, *no*! There was no mistaking that mocking voice.
It rasped across her nerves like sandpaper as a tall
figure stepped away from the Land Cruiser.

'All set, Claude?' he asked, then grasped the edge of
the door and swung up beside Bernadette without
waiting for a reply, a duffle bag hanging from one hand
and a pack slung on his back. He was dressed in
camouflage this morning, his starched trouser legs
bloused over the tops of gleaming paratrooper boots.

'Planning a war, Colonel?' Bernadette asked drily.

Cool grey eyes came to rest on her, blankly
inscrutable. 'Since you ask, no,' he murmured in a
growl that couldn't have carried more than a foot or
two. 'I leave the planning to the people who get paid to
do it. Execution's my field.'

Before that had fully sunk in he turned his head, his
gaze unerringly singling out Kaisi and Amira for a brief
but thorough inspection. 'Ladies,' he acknowledged
curtly, and then called: 'Let's get cracking, Claude,'
over his shoulder and ducked inside.

At least he wasn't inflicting his presence on them,
Bernadette realised with relief as he headed straight for

the cockpit. And then Claude Dorleac was beside her, reaching for the heavy sliding door, and all she had time for was a quick wave to Timothy before she had to step back out of the way and find a seat on one of the benches.

Her regret that there weren't any windows from which to view the sunrise vanished as the three huge engines kicked into life and the smaller girls had to be soothed and reassured that their incredible noise didn't signal impending doom. And then they began to move, and she was kept busy making sure everyone held on to the looped straps above their heads, so that none of them was thrown on to the crates stacked with military precision down the centre of the hold as the plane lurched across the uneven ground.

'Everybody okay back there?'

Forrester's question rose above the roar of the engines as soon as they were airborne.

'Peachy keen, thanks,' Bernadette called back sarcastically. 'We're having a tea party. Care to join us?'

Through the cockpit door she saw his head swivel to direct a cool stare at her from the co-pilot's seat. One dark brow hooked in sardonic question before he faced the instrument panel again.

She knew her cheeks were flushed, mainly from shame for succumbing to the petty urge to dig at him like that. The surprised frown Mrs Althoff gave her when their eyes met across the crates increased her discomfort.

'That wasn't like you,' the older woman chided. 'He *is* the man who arranged for M. Dorleac to fly us home, isn't he?'

Bernadette nodded, not wanting to raise her voice and be overheard by the two in the cockpit.

'Well, I should think you'd show a little more gratitude. I realise this isn't exactly first class, but we *are* on the way home, primarily thanks to his efforts.'

The rebuke was delivered in Mrs Althoff's best public speaking voice, which Bernadette had no doubt carried quite clearly to the Colonel's ears. The suspicion was confirmed a second later, when his lazy response boomed back to them.

'It was no trouble, ma'am, no trouble at all,' he asserted, and then his head swung around to flash a charming smile at Mrs Althoff and spear Bernadette with a wickedly amused look. 'Glad to do it,' he added smoothly, and then faced forward again, laughing softly at something Claude said to him in French.

Phoney! Bernadette thought as she saw the contented smile on Mrs Althoff's face. He might be able to pull the wool over the eyes of a kind-hearted widow lady, but he didn't have *her* fooled for a minute! That aw-shucks charm was just an act; inside he was a hardened cynic, always looking out for Number One, and heaven help anyone who got in his way or crossed him. She settled back and got as comfortable as was possible on the narrow bench, and stared fixedly at the crate in front of her, her small face pinched with disapproval.

They'd been in the air about an hour and a half when Forrester left the cockpit and walked straight to where Bernadette was sitting, his tall frame stooped to avoid hitting his head on the roof. When he reached her, he sank down on his haunches and looked up at her.

'How's everybody holding up?'

'Fairly well,' she answered coolly. 'They're generally well-behaved girls, Colonel, they won't give you any trouble.'

'I wasn't implying they would.' His eyes seemed to glow in the dim light as they lingered on her face, and then he turned his head to look at the girls, some of whom were slumped against their neighbours in sleep. Mrs Althoff, too, had dozed off and was snoring softly.

'We'll be setting down in a little over half an hour. I suggest you make sure they're all awake. It'll be a rough landing, and if they're asleep they could be thrown around and injured.'

'How good of you to be concerned,' Bernadette said flatly.

His eyes narrowed as they returned to her face. 'Still sore about last night, are you?' he drawled, then lifted one shoulder carelessly. 'All right, I misinterpreted the situation. I thought you were coming on to me, and I was more than willing. Don't pretend it was the first time you've had to fend a man off, Bernie,' he mocked with lazy amusement. 'You're too much woman not to have had your share of passes.'

She pointedly ignored his backhanded attempt at flattery. 'Are all these crates yours, Colonel?' she asked, and noted his momentary surprise.

'No, I'm only delivering them. Why do you ask?'

'I'd like to know whether any of the contents is liable to blow us sky high when we make this "rough landing", that's why!' Her voice had dropped to a whisper, but it was tense with suppressed anger. 'I'm neither illiterate nor stupid, Colonel. Those crates were shipped by weapons' manufacturers and munitions factories. A couple of them came all the way from the States. Is any of your *cargo* likely to ignite or explode in our faces?'

'Damn!' The expletive itself was a soft explosion. He raked a hand through his hair and then scowled up at her, tight-lipped and obviously angered by her discovery. 'The answer to your question is no,' he grated. 'There's no possibility of either spontaneous combustion or detonation. I wouldn't have agreed to bring you along if there was the slightest chance any of you might be hurt.'

'*You* wouldn't have agreed!' Bernadette demanded incredulously.

'That's right! As you so cleverly deduced, this is *my* cargo. Claude had already contracted to transport it and me, and he normally only takes on one job at a time.'

'Well, I wish he'd followed standard procedure *this* time!' Bernadette whispered fiercely. 'I promise you, Colonel, if anything happens to these girls, I'll hold you personally responsible!'

'Nothing's going to happen, dammit!' he growled. 'I told you, there's absolutely no danger from anything in those crates.'

'Oh, really? Don't take me for a fool, Colonel! No danger from guns and ammunition, and probably

explosives, too? I suppose you're going to use them to
build roads, or maybe a new hydro-electric plant?'

His face closed up and his voice went hard; hard and
cold with anger. 'What I do with them is none of your
damned business, Miss Chapman. Now I suggest you
begin waking your charges, who *are* your business, and
keep your sanctimonious little nose out of mine!'

He rose and was headed towards the front of the
plane before she could respond to his cutting words,
leaving Bernadette shaken and outraged. She took a
couple of deep breaths and then began gently waking
the girls, preparing them for the landing they should be
making in twenty-five minutes or so.

Only they came down a lot sooner than that.

Everything happened so fast that only later could
Bernadette realise how lucky they'd been, and appreciate
both the swiftness of Sam Forrester's reflexes and the
degree of Claude Dorleac's skill as a flyer.

She had just jostled Mrs Althoff awake and was on
her way back to her place on the other side of the hold,
when suddenly the whole plane seemed to shudder and
the floor was tilting beneath her feet. She clutched at
one of the heavy crates at the same time Claude
Dorleac started to swear vehemently in French:
something about the engineers of McDonnell Douglas
having been high on drugs and in the process of having
intimate relations with sheep—or was it goats—when
they designed his engines. If she hadn't been utterly
terrified, she might have burst out laughing.

Then suddenly Forrester was in the hold, scooping up
Lizbeth and Tumara and rapping out orders for Patrice
and Melissande to grab the two sisters and bring them
to the rear. Bernadette understood his reasoning at
once: if they crashed, the cargo would slide forward and
possibly to the side on impact. Unfortunately, both she
and Mrs Althoff had taken places towards the front of
the hold, and with the floor pitching and heaving
under them it was all but impossible to make their way
to the rear.

'Get up to the cockpit and strap yourself in!'

Bernadette looked around at the brusque command,

and saw that Forrester had reached the pale and trembling headmistress. *'Go!'* he bellowed as he swung her up in his arms, and Bernadette didn't wait to be told again.

She staggered to the door, and actually had one hand on the bulkhead when something slammed into her from behind and she was thrown forward.

When awareness returned, she was being carried in a pair of strong, sinewy arms. Her eyes fluttered open to discover a bright blue sky overhead, and—much closer—the sternly forbidding features of Colonel Sam Forrester.

'The girls——?' she said weakly, and his cool gaze instantly dropped to her face.

'They're all fine. A few cuts and bruises, nothing serious. And before you ask, your Mrs Alton is——'

'Althoff,' Bernadette corrected in a feeble voice.

'Whatever. She's unharmed, as well. Now shut up and save your strength until I can determine how serious your injuries are.'

'My injuries?' Had she been hurt? She couldn't remember a thing after he'd yelled at her to go to the cockpit.

'One of the crates hit you. You've got a small cut on the head and a possible concussion, at the very least.'

His tone was brisk and impersonal, but when he laid her on soft grass in the shade of a tree he was unexpectedly gentle. Bernadette blushed fiery red at his thorough examination as he checked for broken bones or damaged muscles, but he didn't take any notice of her embarrassment.

'You are one lucky lady,' he murmured as he refastened her blouse. 'No broken ribs, though I imagine you'll be as sore as hell for a few days.'

Next he went over her head, his lean fingers slipping through the silky hair to probe her scalp for any more cuts or lumps, then checked for blood at her ears and nose. 'Close your eyes,' he instructed, then: 'Okay, now open them.' He peered into first one wide violet orb and then the other. 'How many fingers do you see?' he asked as he held up two in front of her face.

'Two, both grubby,' Bernadette answered curtly.

'One has a scratch just below the first knuckle. Satisfied?'

Forrester's mouth quirked in that slanting half smile that was becoming familiar and he rocked back on his heels. 'I guess you'll do. No dizziness or nausea?'

'None, just a slight headache. Can I get up now, Dr Forrester?'

He ignored her slightly patronising amusement. 'No. Stay there. You could have a delayed reaction.' He rose to his feet in one smooth movement. 'I'll send the girls and Mrs Whozit over to wait with you while we assess the damage to the plane.'

Mrs Althoff and the girls came running across the field in which they'd made the forced landing as soon as he gave the okay, the four youngest girls throwing themselves on Bernadette in joyful relief.

'We thought you were dead,' Lizbeth confessed, and the others nodded solemnly.

'Colonel Forrester called and called to you, but you didn't answer,' added Melissande.

'And then he started swearing,' Tumara put in, her eyes wide.

'Boy, did he ever!' Patrice grinned as she contributed the last comment. 'If Mrs A hadn't already been in shock, his language would have put her there.'

'I wouldn't be so sure of that, Patrice,' Mrs Althoff remarked as she arrived, flushed and out of breath. She shooed the girls out of the way to reach Bernadette's side. 'I haven't lived fifty-seven years without hearing the occasional swear word. And considering the circumstances, I think Colonel Forrester's lapse can be excused. You gave us all a fright, dear,' she said to Bernadette with a worried frown. 'Are you sure you're quite all right?'

'Fine, except for a doozy of a headache. The Colonel says I cut my head on something when I fell.'

'Yes, but it could have been much worse.' Mrs Althoff opened the metal first-aid kit she'd brought and took out cotton and antiseptic. 'From the way he was carrying on, we thought you'd broken your neck, at the very least.'

The observation was tinged with dry amusement. Personally, Bernadette couldn't imagine Sam Forrester 'carrying on' about anything, but she refrained from saying so.

'I must have landed in the cockpit. Couldn't M. Dorleac have told him I'd just had a knock on the head?'

'I'm afraid not, dear. He was unconscious himself for several minutes, in addition to which the crate that sent you flying was blocking the door. For a while I thought the Colonel meant to take it apart with his bare hands, but he eventually moved it enough to squeeze through. There, that should do it, I think. The skin was barely broken, no need for a bandage.'

A little later both men came across the field, and Bernadette watched their faces closely as they approached, trying to guess what news they carried. Forrester's expression gave nothing away, as usual. Claude Dorleac, on the other hand, was smiling. She breathed a silent sigh of relief.

'Well, how bad is it?' Mrs Althoff asked briskly.

'Not as bad as it could have been, but bad enough.' The Colonel's eyes fixed on Bernadette's pale face as he took it upon himself to answer. 'The fuel lines to two of the engines are clogged. I'm afraid we're stuck here until we can free them, and that'll probably be sometime this evening. Since there's no question of taking off after dark, we won't be leaving until tomorrow morning.'

'Also,' their pilot put in with a grimace, 'the third engine was running raggedly even before the trouble developed with the other two. I'm afraid we cannot rely on it for takeoff.'

Something in his voice, combined with his darting glance at Forrester, sent a tingle of reaction down Bernadette's spine.

'Sabotage?' she asked softly as she looked into the Colonel's eyes.

'Could be.' He didn't hesitate over the reply, nor did he seem overly concerned by the possibility.

'I would say it was likely, Mademoiselle,' Dorleac

murmured as he squatted in front of her. 'The plane was left unguarded in the field outside Mombasa all night. My pre-flight check turned up nothing suspicious, but . . .' he gave an expressive Gallic shrug, 'for a man who knows his business, it would not be difficult to conceal the evidence of sabotage until we were in the air, and then it would be too late. I do not wish to frighten you——'

'I'm not frightened,' Bernadette interrupted softly. 'It's a little late for that, now.' She lifted accusing eyes to Forrester. 'It would have been someone who knew about your cargo, wouldn't it?' she asked with an icy calm.

He didn't answer, but then he didn't have to.

'No danger at all, right, Colonel?' she said in a tone that carried only to him and the Frenchman, who was frowning as he looked from one of them to the other.

Forrester's mouth tightened almost imperceptibly, but he still didn't respond.

'Claude, we'd better get to work on those fuel lines,' he said flatly, then turned on his heel and walked away with long, swinging strides. The pilot cast Bernadette a quizzical glance, and then followed.

Throughout the afternoon and on into evening they worked, both stripped to the waist under the African sun, sweat pouring down their bodies to darken the waists of their trousers and glisten like oil on their skins.

The girls and Mrs Althoff succumbed to the heat midway through the afternoon and fell asleep sprawled on the grass, so there was little for Bernadette to do but watch the two men. Their conversation was limited to monosyllables, few and far between, and either consciously or unconsciously spoken in French. The language should have sounded clumsy or discordant when spoken in Forrester's normal growl, but it didn't. Instead, his terse questions and muttered comments came out sounding like impatient love words, deliciously sexy; as if the engine he was working on was a temperamental woman whose pretence at reluctance might irritate him, but for whom he would play the game because of the reward he knew he'd receive at the end of it.

Bernadette was mildly amazed at herself for such erotic thoughts. Good heavens, the heat must be getting to her! She didn't even *like* the man, and here she was fantasising about his behaviour in bed with some nonexistent woman.

It was because she'd never seen such a glorious male specimen, she decided with a detached appreciation as she let her eyes linger on his gleaming torso. He was obviously in the peak of condition, lean and tough, his arms and chest and shoulders well-muscled but not grotesquely so, his stomach hard and flat. His movements were smooth, unhurried looking, like the movements of a well-oiled machine. Both he and the Frenchman seemed tireless, immune to the heat and humidity as they laboured over the mammoth engines.

After a while Bernadette grew restive. Just sitting and watching while other people worked was a rotten way to pass an afternoon. She checked to see that the others were still sleeping, then strolled over to the plane.

'Can I do anything to help?'

She addressed the question to Dorleac, but it was Forrester who answered.

'Go inside and fetch a jug of water from the locker behind the pilot's seat.'

That was it. No please or thank you—he didn't even look up as he spoke. Bernadette's mouth compressed and she turned away without a word. It was a good thing she was young and limber, she thought as she hauled herself up through the door and slithered around the crate still partially blocking the cockpit.

'Thanks. You should have gone up directly from underneath,' Forrester said when she returned and handed him the plastic jug.

She stooped to peer under the belly of the plane and saw an open hatch cover.

'Is that how you brought me out?' she asked as she straightened.

He lifted an arm to wipe the sweat from his brow before it could run into his eyes. 'It was either that or throw you over my shoulder, and I had no idea how badly you were injured.'

'It wasn't a criticism,' she said quietly as he recapped the jug and tossed it to Claude on the other wing.

'That makes for a nice change,' he drawled. 'How's your head?'

Bernadette silently counted to ten and shielded her eyes with a hand as she squinted up at him, standing spread-legged on the wing above her.

'If I've seemed hypercritical, Colonel, it's because the safety of the girls is my responsibility, and I don't take my responsibilities lightly. They could have been killed this morning, and you would have been indirectly to blame. Do you deny that?'

'I guess I ought to be grateful for that "indirectly",' he drawled, then deliberately turned his back and dropped to his knees to resume whatever he'd been doing to the engine. Bernadette's temper started to sizzle at his apparent indifference.

'I take it no denial is forthcoming,' she murmured.

Forrester's broad shoulders rose and fell in a sigh of impatience, and then he swivelled on one knee to frown down at her.

'All right, Miss High and Mighty Chapman,' he muttered. '*If* anyone had been seriously injured, the blame would have been mine. At least indirectly,' he added with a nasty little smile. 'Satisfied?'

Bernadette's nod was a stiff inclination of her head that seemed to have the irritating effect of amusing him.

'Good. Now why don't you get back in the shade where you belong and let me get on with my work, hmm?'

Before she could think up a retort Bernadette was presented with his back again. She felt like a child who'd been chastised and then sent to her room as she recrossed the field and settled down under a tree, her knees tucked up to her chest. The man was absolutely impossible—arrogant, condescending, the ultimate chauvinist. Hadn't anyone told him this was the latter half of the twentieth century, for heaven's sake!

She leaned back against the tree trunk and closed her

eyes with a slight frown. Her head was throbbing, and the heat seemed to be sapping her energy. She'd just sit here for a while and rest . . .

'Come on, Bernie, haul it out.'

The toe of a boot prodded her backside, and Bernadette heard the giggles of children, dimly, through the receding fog of sleep.

'Up and at 'em, girl, if you want any supper.'

That voice! Merciful heavens, was there no escape from it? It rolled down at her like thunder, and she obstinately kept her eyes closed, feigning sleep, curled on her side like an infant.

'Bernie?'

The lazy amusement was suddenly gone from The Voice, and it was also suddenly much closer—right above her, in fact. Bernadette forced herself to remain limp, her muscles slack, knowing those sharp grey eyes were watching, would instantly spot any tensing or other sign of wakefulness.

A hard, square palm was placed against her cheek and The Voice softened, became almost concerned as it repeated the disgusting corruption of her name.

'Bernie? Can you hear me, girl? Open your eyes.'

She lay perfectly still, quelling the laughter within her. It proved to be quite a chore when one eyelid was gently pried open by his thumb and his frowning face loomed over her, filling her vision. She conquered the impulse to giggle and stared blindly straight ahead.

He swore softly as he let her eye fall shut. 'Bernie, honey, wake up. Come on, there's a good girl, open your eyes for me,' he coaxed, his hands turning her on to her back and gently shaking her by the shoulders.

Bernadette was convinced that in another minute she was going to burst out laughing and give the game away. She played for time by allowing her eyelids to flutter weakly, her thick lashes like struggling moths against her pale cheeks.

'That's it! Open your eyes, sweetheart.'

Sweetheart! She nearly snorted in hilarity as her lashes swept up to treat him to the sight of wide, blankly questioning pools of violet.

'Bernie?' Forrester murmured with an uncertain frown.

She blinked, then said in a soft, confused little voice: 'Who are you?'

He was clearly dumbfounded for a moment. 'Who——?'

'And ... and where am I?' she added with just a hint of alarm as her eyes darted to the leafy branches above and the open field beyond him. Actually, she was checking to see if Mrs Althoff and the girls were hovering anxiously. Thankfully they were nowhere to be seen; she didn't think she could have kept up the act if they'd been looking on.

'Listen!' Forrester's strong fingers gripped her chin to bring her attention back to him, his frown deepening. 'Do you remember who *you* are? What's your name?'

She hesitated for a convincing second. 'You called me Bernie, didn't you? It's ... it's Bernadette ... I think. But——'

'And what do you do? Where do you live?'

'I ... teach school, don't I? In ... in Bulawayo, Zimbabwe. But ... oh, please, tell me who you are and what I'm doing here with you, Mr ... Mr ...'

'You really don't remember?' he challenged. At her puzzled shake of the head, he muttered, 'Looks like shock tactics are in order,' under his breath.

It happened so fast Bernadette didn't have time to prepare, either mentally or physically. True, he'd kissed her before, but it had been nothing whatsoever like this. His mouth was so warm and tender, coaxing, gentle on hers, his breath flowing into her mouth as he exhaled on a sigh.

'Does this ring any bells?' he murmured against her lips.

'I——'

Whatever else she'd been about to say was lost as he kissed her again. His gentleness took her by surprise, and without being fully aware that she was doing it she started kissing him back, just as gently.

His hand curved to fit her waist as he murmured something unintelligible, his long fingers sliding with masterful confidence to her ribcage. Bernadette was fully aware that the game had gone further than she ever intended, that it was sheer lunacy to keep playing, and that if she didn't put a halt to things—and soon—she was in imminent danger of losing control of the situation. Why, then, were her hands inching up his bare chest, through the springy hair curling there, unquestionably heading for his neck?

His skin was like warm silk, slightly damp, firm and smooth under her palms. That lean, tough body felt every bit as good as it looked, Bernadette decided as her fingers spread on his shoulders. It took a determined effort of will to push against him.

'Please!' she gasped as she twisted her head to one side, then worried that he might take the breathless plea as encouragement.

His uneven breath fanned her face as he hesitated, his thumb nudging the underside of her breast. She could feel the touch of his eyes, and reluctantly turned her head to meet them.

'You're supposed to say: "Oh yes, it's all coming back to me now",' he mocked in a husky drawl. Then, when Bernadette only gazed up at him anxiously, one of his thick brows lifted in wry disappointment. 'No?'

'Would you please let me up?' she whispered. The horrible thought had just occurred that Mrs Althoff might have witnessed the kiss. *Make that: kisses*, her conscience nagged. Also, unless she was mistaken—and she knew she wasn't—his hand had crept up a centimetre or two and showed no sign of retreating. It wasn't so much that she minded the intimacy of his touch; it was that she *didn't* mind . . . and that worried her.

'Please,' she asked again, very softly.

Forrester's eyes narrowed as he registered her apprehension, and then suddenly he was on his feet, reaching down to her.

'Easy, now,' he started to say as Bernadette placed her hands in his, but she was too eager to get off her back to pay him any attention.

The drunken way she swayed upon coming upright was no act. Her face blanched and she closed her eyes against the sick dizziness which swept up from her stomach, then slumped against him as his arms came around her to lend support.

'Dammit, Bernie, I tried to tell you,' he muttered irritably. 'Are you all right?'

Bernadette nodded cautiously, afraid she'd throw up all over him if she tried to speak.

He glanced down at her chalky face, the way her eyes were squeezed shut. 'Like hell. Just stay there for a little while. Don't move. It'll pass in a minute.'

While Bernadette rested against him and tried not to be sick, inspiration struck. When she thought she could open her eyes without sending the universe into a tailspin, she took a couple of deep breaths and lifted her face to him.

'Colonel Forrester?' she said with a bewildered frown, then sucked in her breath and pushed away from him indignantly. 'You never let a chance go by, do you?'

His brow puckered as he folded his arms over his chest. 'Back to your charming self, I see,' he muttered. 'At least you remembered my name. I guess that's something.'

'I'm not likely to forget it,' Bernadette retorted sharply. 'Not when every time I turn around, you're making a grab for me. Do you make a habit of this sort of thing, Colonel, or have you just taken a dislike to me, personally?'

His mouth thinned as he stared at her with those cool grey eyes, and then a thought seemed to occur out of the blue. His brows drew together until they almost met over the bridge of his nose, giving him a faintly menacing look.

'What's the last thing you remember—before you felt dizzy?'

Bernadette's reaction was perfect: impatient, but just a bit uncertain. 'I fail to see what that has to do with anything, but since you ask, I sat down against that tree and must have dozed off. I guess it was the heat. I do seem to recall feeling woozy all of a sudden,' she improvised in a burst of inspired creativity.

'Delayed reaction,' Forrester murmured, nodding, and then a note of wry amusement entered his deep voice as he added: 'That explains it, then.'

'I beg your pardon?' Bernadette barely kept a straight face, and hoped she wasn't turning a guilty shade of pink.

'Never mind,' he said on a sigh. Then suddenly he was all business. 'I came to tell you supper's ready. Field rations, I'm afraid, but nourishing and filling. At least the girls won't go to bed on empty stomachs. Can you make it to the plane on your own, or should I carry you?'

Bernadette glanced at him sharply, but there was no telltale bulge at his cheek. 'I think I can manage, thank you,' she replied as she walked past him.

They hadn't gone ten feet when she felt his fingers in her hair. She stopped and gave him a hard look.

'Grass,' he explained soberly. 'And a twig,' as he reached up to tug it loose.

'Thank you so much,' Bernadette said insincerely before she continued on towards the plane.

'You're ever so welcome,' Forrester mocked. 'I never let a chance go by, remember. Besides, we wouldn't want anyone to think you've been rolling around on the ground with me, now would we?'

Her cheeks flamed, but she kept her eyes straight ahead and her voice cool.

'I seriously doubt anyone would think that, Colonel. At least not anyone who knows me.'

'Now *that* I can believe.'

He didn't speak again until they were halfway across the field, and then he reached out to grasp her arm and draw her to a halt.

'Do you mind!' Bernadette complained as she withdrew from his touch.

Forrester's mouth pulled down at the corners and he gave her one of his narrow-eyed stares.

'I wasn't intending to throw you down and rape you,' he growled. 'We've got a slight problem.'

Bernadette's irritation was instantly forgotten. 'What is it? More trouble with the plane?'

'In a way.' He glanced towards the hulking shape at the far end of the field, his brow furrowed in what could only be called a scowl. 'Claude couldn't get the third engine running—at all. That means he'll only have two for takeoff in the morning. There's no way two engines can lift the weight he's carrying.'

'Which means?' Bernadette thought she could guess, but she wanted the satisfaction of hearing him say it.

Forrester heaved an aggravated sigh. 'We'll have to ditch the cargo.'

'Pity,' she commented flatly.

His head swung around and he nailed her with a piercing look. 'Along with two passengers,' he murmured with sadistic pleasure.

Bernadette hid her shock well. 'You and me, I suppose?' she said calmly, while her stomach dropped to her ankles.

'That was the plan, yes.' Forrester's brows drew together again and his mouth pursed slightly. 'But now I'm not so sure. How does your head feel?'

Her shoulders lifted in a shrug. 'I'm barely aware of it,' she lied gamely.

'Still—it might be best to leave one of the others behind, just in case. If you were to have a cerebral haemorrhage out here——'

'Don't be ridiculous!' Bernadette scoffed. 'I'm not going to have any such thing. Besides, who else would you choose? A fifty-seven-year-old woman who's recovering from a bout of malaria, or a couple of the girls—it would take two of them to make up the weight, wouldn't it? No, I'll stay.'

He heard her out silently, his glum expression saying she was only repeating his own reasoning but that he still wasn't satisfied with the only obvious solution. Then he took her arm again to urge her towards the plane.

'We'll see,' he murmured.

'I'm staying,' Bernadette repeated with quiet determination.

Forrester's mouth thinned, but he didn't argue. He couldn't, she thought grimly. What was there to say?

She was the only logical choice, and they both knew it. When the plane took off tomorrow morning, the two of them would be left behind with the cargo . . .

Alone . . .

In the heart of the African interior.

CHAPTER THREE

CLAUDE DORLEAC didn't appear to have suffered any lasting effects from having been slammed into his own instrument panel hard enough to knock him out, Bernadette thought as she watched him.

They were all seated in an irregular circle in the shadow of the plane, eating the field rations Colonel Forrester had unpacked. He'd been right, she admitted as she forced down another spoonful of canned beef: the food might have the flavour and consistency of wallpaper paste, but at least it was filling. *Too* filling. After several mouthfuls, it lay in her stomach like a rock. She caught the young pilot grinning at her as she set the can of beef aside.

'Cordon bleu it's not, *n'est-ce pas*?' he remarked.

'Not quite,' she agreed with a smile. 'But since I've eaten much worse, I won't complain.'

She was aware of Forrester's watchful eyes on them as the Frenchman moved to sit beside her.

'You have aroused my curiosity, Mademoiselle—when and where have you eaten food worse than this?'

He was relaxed and friendly tonight, flirtatious, but in a nice way. Bernadette hugged her knees to her chest as she answered.

'Belfast is one place that comes to mind.'

His brows shot up in surprise. 'Northern Ireland? You have been there?'

'Mmm, a couple of years ago. The World Health Organisation was conducting a study of nutritional deficiencies, and they needed a qualified librarian to catalogue the research data. I was doing similar work in the medical library of a large university hospital back home, so an old family friend who thought I'd be interested suggested me for the job.'

'This friend—he was someone with WHO?' Dorleac was clearly intrigued.

41

Bernadette smiled. 'No. He was Archbishop Mahoney.'

A stunned silence followed, and then Dorleac murmured in awe: 'You know the archbishop, himself?'

'As I said, he's an old friend of the family. He and my uncle went into the priesthood together, and my older brother serves on his staff,' Bernadette explained absently.

She'd noticed that several of the girls were yawning and nodding sleepily. When she excused herself to shepherd them off to bed, he rose to help. Forrester had made it graphically clear why it was imperative that they spend the hours of darkness inside the plane. They wouldn't be risking a fire near it since so much high octane aircraft fuel had been used cleaning the engines, and he and Dorleac were too tired to maintain a night-long vigil. Bernadette was extremely grateful for the security of the cargo hold, with its thick metal skin and heavy door. This was one night she didn't expect to feel at all claustrophobic.

Mrs Althoff was clearly exhausted, and turned in with the girls; but since it was still several hours before her usual bedtime Bernadette elected to go back out for a while. She hopped down from the open door and found the two men talking in French, their voices subdued, in the shadows under the wing. As she approached, Forrester muttered a terse instruction she couldn't quite catch and turned towards her.

'You should be resting.'

'I'm not tired,' she replied coolly, irritated by his penchant for giving orders instead of making suggestions, like any normal, civilised man.

No, that wasn't right, she amended reluctantly. Despite his often boorish behaviour, she couldn't really label him uncivilised. He just operated according to his own code, and the rules of polite society be damned.

He stared at her silently a second or two, and then shrugged. 'Suit yourself.' Then, apparently dismissing her completely, he turned back to the Frenchman. 'Think I'll have a quick look around.'

Some kind of message was concealed within the

casual statement, Bernadette felt sure, but she was at a loss to interpret it. Her lips pursed as she stuck the tips of her fingers into her front pockets, attentive but silent. Forrester bent to pick up something propped against the wing strut, and when he straightened there was a deadly looking rifle in his hand. Bernadette felt chilled as she watched the easy, familiar way he handled the weapon. And then he turned and walked away without so much as a glance in her direction.

She didn't realise she was staring after him until Claude Dorleac spoke.

'You disturb him,' he said softly. 'Even more, I believe, than he disturbs you.'

Bernadette's mouth tilted wryly. 'But I don't think in quite the same way.'

'No.' His wicked grin was amused. 'Not yet, anyway.' Before she could decide how to take that, he added thoughtfully, 'He has never met a woman quite like you before.'

'Well that makes us even,' Bernadette retorted, 'because I've certainly never met a man like him.'

The young pilot shrugged. 'That is because there are none. He is one of a kind. Shall we sit on the wing for a while—it will not be fully dark for another thirty minutes or so.'

They sat in companionable silence for a while, their legs dangling over the edge of the wing while dusk deepened and the night sounds that were uniquely Africa began to become noticeable.

'Such a wildly beautiful country,' Bernadette murmured as she gazed at the solid-looking wall of trees ringing the field and listened to the occasional chirp or plaintive cry from beyond them.

'*Oui*. She is like a fascinating woman—always changing, holding a man's interest with her unpredictability.'

'Ah yes, and you know all about women, don't you?' Bernadette teased, tongue in cheek.

He laughed, a soft, pleasant sound. 'Not *all*, certainly. But having grown up with five older sisters, more than most men, I expect.'

That led to a discussion of their families. It turned out that both of them were the only non-practising Catholics among their relations, and as such a constant source of concern to their mothers.

'They all expected me to become a priest. *Mon Dieu*, can you imagine?'

Bernadette laughingly admitted that she couldn't.

'I felt it was enough that two of my sisters had become nuns,' he explained with a shrug. 'But *ma mere* was very upset with me for a long time after I left home. It was only when I flew a doctor-priest and three nursing sisters out of their mission in the middle of a tribal uprising that she finally forgave me.'

'I should think she would,' Bernadette murmured softly.

He grinned. 'You are impressed. And so you should be. It was an act of supreme bravery and selflessness which undoubtedly earned me a place in Heaven— without having to forego any of life's wicked pleasures.'

It was impossible to take him seriously, when he so obviously didn't, himself. They talked on, each discovering a friend in the other, sitting on the wing of a thirty-year-old airplane parked in a field somewhere north of Zambia.

Bernadette told him how she'd once seriously considered becoming a nun, herself, when she was twelve. The ambition lasted almost a year, until she discovered boys and eye shadow at the same time and realised what she'd be giving up. He laughed, and she laughed with him. Neither was aware of the tall, still man watching silently from the shadows under the trees. If they'd looked in that direction, they might have noticed the glowing tip of a long, thin cheroot as he drew on it deeply.

For the second day in a row they were all awake and stirring before dawn. The men unloaded the heavy crates one by one, then lugged them into the concealing shelter of the trees and covered them with camouflaging tarps.

While Forrester assured himself that his precious

cargo was hidden from prying eyes—and who in the world did he think would be likely to stumble across it, anyway?—Claude returned to the plane to make his pre-flight check.

'Everything all right?' Bernadette asked as she stuck her head into the cockpit.

He looked up with a smile. 'A-okay, to borrow a phrase from your astronauts. Sit with me for a moment,' he invited, indicating the co-pilot's seat. 'I wanted a word with you before we leave.'

Bernadette frowned at his uncharacteristic gravity as she slid into the leather bucket beside him. 'Why, is anything wrong?'

Claude didn't answer until he'd hooked the clipboard holding his checklist on to the side of his seat.

'At the moment, no,' he murmured, then looked into her face with a sombre expression. 'Perhaps I am only . . . how do you say it . . . borrowing trouble.'

'You're worried about leaving me behind,' Bernadette guessed, and he nodded. She slowly folded her hands in her lap, considering just what that implied.

'You obviously have a high regard for Colonel Forrester. You like him, but more important, you trust him. Yet you don't like leaving us alone together.' She looked him squarely in the eye. 'Tell me about him, Claude. All you know,' she asked quietly.

It wasn't a lot, and yet it was everything. He was British by birth, but had lived in Africa almost all his life. The years of his adolescence had been spent in Kenya, during the period marked by the hatred and barbaric violence known as the Mau Mau uprising. By the time the horror began in the Congo, he was a twenty-one-year-old lieutenant in the British Army, assigned to duty with the Nato forces sent there to halt the terrorism. Since then he had served as a member of the Special Forces in various trouble spots around the globe, retiring early six years ago, at the age of thirty-eight. Claude was deliberately vague about Forrester's activities during the last six years, saying only that he occasionally offered his services and expertise to old friends.

'Has he ever been married?' she asked impulsively. For all that he'd provided a lot of information, he hadn't really told her anything about the man, himself.

Claude gave her a wry smile. 'Not to my knowledge. To him, a commitment of that magnitude would be more terrifying than anything he might face in the jungle or on a battlefield.'

'Women make for a pleasant diversion now and then, but God forbid he should get saddled with one for life,' she commented wryly.

'Exactly.' Claude's smooth forehead suddenly furrowed in concern. 'He has no great respect or liking for females, and the two of you already seem to have got off to a bad start, Bernadette. I would advise you not to antagonise him. It could be dangerous.'

She frowned back at him. 'You're not suggesting he'd turn violent on me, are you?'

The young Frenchman's mouth tilted, his half smile amused. 'Not in the way you mean. His instinct for survival is very highly developed, and I have no doubt that he will protect you from any outside threat. What concerns me is that *he* might become a threat to you, if you continue to provoke him as you have been doing.'

Bernadette looked into his eyes and knew that he'd witnessed the scene under the trees yesterday. She flushed with embarrassment.

'I do not mean to alarm you,' he said in reassurance. 'Only to give a friendly warning. Sam is not a man to play games with, Bernadette. He always come out the winner.'

'I can believe that,' she muttered, then sighed. 'I swear, Claude, I have no intention of "provoking" him, at least not that way.'

He grinned again. 'Intentional or not, you do. You are an extremely provocative woman. But if you will only play it cool, stay aloof and reserved, you need not fear his unwanted attentions. Sam Forrester would never force himself on a woman.'

That was something else she had no trouble believing. With his rugged good looks and marvellous physique, not to mention the aura of mystery and danger which clung to him, women would probably line up to throw themselves at his feet. Well, she had no intention of taking a place in that line! Arrogant chauvinists held no attraction for her whatsoever, and she'd make damned sure Colonel Sam Forrester got that message loud and clear, as soon as they were alone.

As it turned out, he got a different but equally off-putting message, courtesy of Claude Dorleac.

Bernadette had said her goodbyes, receiving emotional hugs and kisses from the girls and an affectionate embrace from Mrs Althoff, who didn't seem nearly as upset about leaving her behind as Bernadette had expected. When she appeared in the doorway, Claude was waiting. He reached up to grasp her waist and lift her down. There was no sign of Forrester. Probably guarding his cargo, she thought with a smile, making sure it isn't confiscated by terrorist chimpanzees.

Without being obvious about it, Claude manoeuvred her away from the cargo door, towards the front of the plane.

'You have said your farewells?'

'Yes.'

'We are ready for takeoff. I want you to go to the far end of the field,' he directed, pointing. 'Stay there until we have cleared the trees. *Comprendez*?'

'*Oui, je comprends.*' Bernadette smiled at his sternness. 'I won't stand in the middle of your runway, I promise.'

Claude bent his head and stared down at his feet, his mouth pursed. An almost palpable tension in his silence made Bernadette's mouth go dry.

'Claude?' she whispered anxiously. 'You *will* clear the trees, won't you?'

His head came up at once, a cocky grin smeared over his face. '*Mais certainement*. Still . . .' He reached up to pull off his flight cap, then clasped it in front of him in both hands. 'Will you offer a small prayer for me—for all of us—Soeur Bernadette?'

His tone was perfectly sober, almost humble, but there was a devilish gleam in his eye. Bernadette didn't know whether she was more relieved or exasperated.

Her own eyes glittered as she took one of his hands in
both of hers, as if to give comfort or reassurance.

'Of course,' she murmured in muted, reverential
tones. *'Dieu vous garde, Monsieur.'*

'Merci, ma belle soeur.' His mouth formed a rakish
grin as his eyes flicked over her. 'I can easily imagine
you in a habit—you have the fragile, innocent beauty
and grace of a saint,' he mocked soberly.

Bernadette slanted him a speaking look, a just-who-
the-hell-do-you-think-you're-kidding look, and then
turned and walked to the spot he'd pointed out. By the
time she reached it he was inside the plane and the two
functional engines were warming up. While she stood
and waited, Forrester came to join her, looking even
more grim than usual. It made Bernadette apprehensive.
What did he know that she didn't?

The clumsy-looking old plane lumbered to the far
end of the field, turned with all the grace of a wallowing
hippo, then just sat there while Claude revved the
engines to their maximum power. The roar was
deafening, making any kind of conversation impossible.

Bernadette's muscles were tensed, her palms damp.
Damn Claude, why had he planted that tiny seed of
doubt in her mind? When he released the brakes and
the shuddering aircraft lunged forward, she impulsively
crossed herself, the gesture more superstitious than
devout.

It was over so quickly she didn't have time to be really
afraid. The plane's undercarriage flirted with the topmost
branches—causing them to flap and wave like arthritic
hands in a wild parody of farewell—but as Claude had
predicted, he cleared the trees with room to spare.

Bernadette turned to the Colonel, a smile of relief
lighting her face. The furious glare he gave back
extinguished it at once, and her forehead creased in a
baffled frown. Good grief, what was he mad about *now*?

'This is yours,' he said tersely, flinging the smaller of
two backpacks at her. She barely got her hands up to
catch it before it slammed into her chest. 'Take care of
it, half our food and the emergency medical supplies are
in there.'

His cold, restrained anger confounded Bernadette. She racked her brain, but couldn't remember doing or saying anything—at least, not recently—that would have set him off again. They hadn't even spoken since he told her to suit herself last night and then walked off into the trees.

She tugged on the military-style canvas pack with its attached, rolled up sleeping bag and buckled the straps, not complaining about the weight when she noticed that his was easily twice as large and straining at the seams. Until now she hadn't questioned what would happen *after* the plane took off without them. She decided it was about time she did.

'Do we really need all this stuff?'

The faint note of challenge in her voice seemed to anger him even more, and she wished she hadn't asked when his head swivelled towards her, his rugged features taut with open contempt.

'All this "stuff", as you put it, is essential equipment and supplies,' he growled. 'You'll be thankful we have it by the time we reach civilisation.'

He turned away to collect a gunbelt made of lightweight webbing, which he strapped around his lean waist. The heavy pistol looked disturbingly natural as it settled against his thigh, weighing the belt down so that it rested on his hip. Bernadette wasn't about to ask if he really needed the gun.

'And how long will that take—to get back to civilisation?' she asked instead.

'That depends on how fast you can walk.' Before she could respond to his sarcasm he was coming towards her, another gunbelt—complete with gun—in his hand.

'This one's yours,' he informed her.

'No.' Bernadette shook her head and backed up a step, her mouth thinning.

'Yes.' His tone was soft, but implacable.

'I won't wear that.'

'I beg to differ. You damn well will.'

She shook her head again, adamant. 'I won't, and you can't——'

He not only could, he did.

'Lesson number one,' he growled as his long fingers deftly buckled the belt over her stomach, causing it to contract sharply in reaction. 'Never tell me I can't, unless you want to see me prove I can.'

Bernadette's eyes met his briefly, then dropped to the small-calibre pistol on her right hip in disgust.

'That was an empty and gratuitous display of your superior strength, Colonel,' she said with a composure she was far from feeling. 'You might force me to wear it, but nothing in this world can make me use it.'

'Not even to save your own life?' he taunted.

'No, not even then.'

'How about to save mine?'

She swallowed, then shook her head. 'I'm sorry, Colonel, but no,' she murmured decisively.

Forrester's lips twisted in a cynical smile. 'I wonder why I'm not surprised. Don't fly into a zealous rage, I don't expect you to use the damned thing,' he sneered. 'Think of it as a deterrent.'

'Is it loaded?' Bernadette demanded, her voice flat.

This time his flickering smile held genuine amusement. 'There's one sure way to find out,' he drawled, then turned his back on her to heft the rifle she'd seen last night and sling it over a shoulder.

'Get a move on, we've got a lot of ground to cover before dark.'

Bernadette decided as she followed him into the trees that he was without doubt the most obnoxious man it had ever been her misfortune to meet, bar none. There were a dozen questions she wanted to ask him—for instance where were they headed and how long would it take to get there?—but the gruelling pace he set didn't allow for even the most rudimentary conversation. He must be nuclear-powered, she thought as she trudged along in his wake, and must assume she was, too. He surely didn't intend to keep up this forced march all day?

But apparently, he did. Around noon he stopped just long enough to dig some jerked beef, dried fruit, and high-protein bars out of his pack, handed half to her, and then strode on. It was midafternoon when he finally decided a rest stop was in order, and by then Bernadette was too exhausted to do more than sink to the ground in a boneless heap.

'Here,' Forrester said, offering a canteen. 'Take small sips, and drink sparingly.'

Arrogant ass, she thought as she snatched the canteen from his hand and lifted it to her parched lips. Didn't he give her credit for any intelligence at all? She'd just about had it with his stoic, macho silence and his damned condescending attitude, and as soon as she got her wind back she'd tell him so. Who the hell did he think he was, Tarzan of the Apes?

'Thank you,' she said stiffly after wetting her mouth and throat. As he took the canteen from her outstretched hand, his eyes narrowed.

'How are you holding up?'

'Remarkably well, considering,' Bernadette retorted, incensed by the thought that he was being patronising. 'If it's not asking too much, would you mind telling me what our destination is? We've been travelling slightly west of south all day, and to my knowledge there's nothing in that direction but forest, scrub, and eventually a desert. The plane went due south. Why aren't we heading in the same direction?'

Forrester's mouth tightened as he heard her out, irritation and impatience evident in his expression.

'Because what they can fly over, we have to hike through,' he answered tersely.

'We're well provisioned, and you're armed to the teeth,' Bernadette pointed out just as tersely.

His tone became nasty as he replied: 'But unfortunately my arsenal doesn't include a rocket launcher or an anti-tank gun.'

Undaunted, she countered, 'Oh, you expect to come across a tank out here, do you?' with wide-eyed innocence.

He seemed to struggle with the urge to throttle her as they glared at one another, she seated on the ground and he squatting on his haunches in front of her.

'We'd better get a few ground rules straight, before

we go any further,' he gritted, his jaw tense. 'My job is to get us both out of here and back to civilisation, alive and unharmed. It's a a job I've done before, and I'm damned good at it. *Your* job is to do whatever the hell I tell you to do, *when* I tell you, exactly the *way* I tell you. You will not question my decisions or my orders, nor will we waste time discussing them. Do I make myself clear?'

Bernadette didn't answer, simply because she couldn't; disbelieving outrage had locked her jaw and stuck her tongue to the roof of her mouth as she stared at him. He couldn't be real, she thought with disgusted contempt.

'I said . . . do I make myself clear?' Forrester repeated softly.

'Oh, yes. Perfectly.' Somehow Bernadette's voice remained steady, even held an insulting indifference that made his lips pinch and a muscle in his cheek jerk.

The enormity of his anger unnerved and confused her. She could *feel* it, emanating from him in waves, and it was a purely personal anger, directed exclusively at her. It wouldn't have all been generated by her presumptuous questioning of his plans; oh, no, this went beyond that, to something else. What? was the question of the hour.

'Why have you taken such an intense dislike to me, Colonel?' she asked with her usual candour, and saw his jaw flex as if he was grinding his teeth. He actually looked ready to explode as he came off the ground like a released spring.

'You've been sniping at me—continually—since the first time we met,' he grated, turning and taking several long strides away from her.

Sniping? Bernadette frowned. From his point of view, she supposed it might have seemed like that. But in all fairness, he'd fired off more than a few rounds, himself.

'I don't think——' she began in her own defence.

'Plus,' he suddenly spun on his heel, his face darkly flushed and rigid with anger, 'there happens to be my aversion to being made a fool of!' The words were literally forced past clenched teeth, and their savagery took Bernadette completely by surprise.

'Made a fool of?' she repeated, frowning. 'How am I supposed to have done that, for heaven's sake?'

'By pretending to be something you're not, for a start!' he shot back furiously.

'I never did!' Her own temper propelled her to her feet, as well, and she faced him defiantly. 'I told you the day you manhandled me into that filthy alley that I was a schoolteacher, which is exactly what I am! How dare you imply I led you to believe I was anything else!'

'Schoolteacher!' He made the word sound like a particularly repugnant species of rodent. 'Oh, yes, I've no doubt you teach school, but that's not your primary vocation, is it . . . *Sister* Bernadette?'

Bernadette's jaw dropped in astonishment, but only for a moment. She couldn't gnaw on her lower lip with her mouth hanging open.

'You . . . overheard, when I was saying goodbye to Claude,' she murmured. Oh Lord, he thought she was a nun. Claude, you idiot!

'It wasn't intentional, I assure you.' The disclaimer was clipped and terse. 'I happened to be standing at the front of the plane, getting our gear together.'

Which Claude had no doubt known. Bernadette silently revised her previous judgment. Oh, Claude, you devious, conniving . . . *angel*! He'd *meant* to leave Forrester with the impression he obviously had, to ensure that she'd be safe from his 'unwanted attentions'.

Keeping her voice steady and her face composed wasn't easy, but she managed . . . just.

'Am I to take it you have something against nuns, Colonel?'

'Of course I bloody well don't have anything against nuns!' he exploded, looking as if he could cheerfully strangle her. 'And I haven't been any bloody kind of colonel for over six years, dammit!'

'There's no need to shout,' Bernadette told him calmly. 'I can hear you perfectly well.' She was suddenly possessed of a peaceful serenity, confident in the knowledge that—thinking what he did—he no longer posed a threat, if he ever had.

'You might have told me!' he accused furiously.
'Christ Almighty, woman, I'd never have——' His
mouth abruptly snapped shut and he spun away,
stalking off into the undergrowth, daring her to follow or
call after him.

She didn't. She made her own visit into the bushes,
and returned to find him standing patiently, smoking a
cigarette. He dropped it and ground it under his heel as
she approached.

'I meant to tell you—keep an eye out for snakes,' he
said, then stooped for her discarded pack and carelessly
tossed it to her.

Bernadette stared at his retreating back as he started
off again, apparently expecting her to follow, and
silently called him all the names she couldn't say aloud.
Not now. Not unless she wanted to abandon the
protective coloration Claude had so thoughtfully
provided her with.

A nun! Oh Lord, how did a nun act—what did she
say, or more important, what *didn't* she say? Bernadette
tried to recall the soft-spoken, black-clad Sisters from
her years at parochial school, but it had been too long
ago; and besides, no *way* could she picture herself as
one of them. Not in a million years!

She came to the reluctant conclusion that it would be
best not to try and play a part. She would just be
herself—as much as she dared—watch her language,
and hope for the best. How long would she have to
keep up the pretence, after all? One day? Two? Surely
they'd reach some kind of town or village before then?

CHAPTER FOUR

BY noon of the following day she'd just about abandoned hope of ever seeing another human being, much less any sort of community. The world they travelled through seemed populated exclusively by insects, reptiles, and repulsive sluglike creatures Bernadette had no desire to identify. And all of them, without exception, were hell-bent on sampling her flesh, or her blood, or both.

Forrester had covered every exposed inch of her skin with a foul-smelling gunk that should have been rank enough to keep Dracula, himself, at bay. The trouble was, the myriad carnivores they encountered didn't appear to possess olfactory organs, and they'd already taken a nip or two before the taste drove them away. To make matters worse, the Colonel seemed immune to the stings and bites, never batting an eye as he brushed the disgusting creatures off his person. *Show off*, Bernadette thought as she sneered at his back and swatted an appallingly large spider from her arm.

She was exhausted, beat, wiped out. The night before, she'd hardly slept a wink. Forrester, damn him, had coolly informed her when she asked that they weren't carrying a tent. After hiking through primordial forests, swamps, and the tortured tangle of undergrowth that went with them all day, she'd thought it wouldn't matter; that if she could just get her miserable body into a prone position on a dry piece of ground, she'd be out like a light.

Not so, she discovered when, bundled into her sleeping bag, the night noises had begun to close in on her. Every soft rustle was a poisonous snake slithering towards her, its sole intent to join her inside the bag. Each grunting cough was a hungry cat on the prowl, whiskers twitching as it searched for a warm-blooded midnight snack. The night had lasted forever, and

moments after she finally slipped into an exhausted
doze, Forrester's hateful voice was growling at her to
rise and shine. She'd been tempted, for just a second
there, to forget her aversion to violence and use the gun
he'd forced her to wear . . . on him.

She had a general idea where they were—very
general, considering the size of the African continent—
although he was being infuriatingly close-mouthed
about their exact location and their ultimate destination.
Still, Bernadette possessed a keen intellect and excellent
deductive reasoning abilities. By the time they paused
for another brief rest stop and freeze-dried lunch, she
had estimated their position to be the eastern Katanga
region of Southern Zaire. As she shrugged out of her
pack, she remarked casually, 'I'm surprised we haven't
come across a coffee or cocoa plantation by now.'

Forrester gave her a sharp, surprised glance and she
repressed a smile that would have looked smug.

'As a matter of fact, we've skirted the outer
boundaries of two,' he muttered as he lit a cigarette,
cupping his hands around the match.

'Why?' The question was also an accusation.

He exhaled a long stream of smoke before answering
coolly, 'Because I don't know the owners. If you need
to answer nature's call, do it now. We won't be
stopping again until we make camp.'

Infuriating, stuck-up pig! Bernadette fumed silently as
she resnapped her jeans and started back for the game
trail they'd been following. It wasn't enough that he
refused to tell her a thing that was going on inside that
rock hard skull of his—treating her like some simple-
minded idiot who couldn't be relied upon to understand
words of more than two syllables! She also had no
privacy whatsoever. Every time she trekked off into the
bushes, he knew exactly why; and to exacerbate her
embarrassment, he was always finished first and waiting
for her patiently. *Oh, to be built like a man*, she thought
enviously, then caught herself up short with a grin.
*Scratch that request, Lord; just chalk it up to mental
fatigue.*

The grin was still playing around her mouth when, a

scant six feet from the trail, a python as big around as her arm and easily eight feet long dropped out of a tree and landed on her shoulders.

Her screams as she twisted and turned, hysterically trying to dislodge the snake, brought Forrester at a run, his pistol in his hand. By the time he reached her, the snake had coiled around Bernadette's ribcage and begun to constrict. Its open mouth was stretching towards her face, and she had both hands clamped around it in a death grip as she struggled to hold it off.

Calmly, his voice low and unconcerned, Forrester told her to hang on to the head, then reholstered his gun and began unwinding the snake from the opposite end. In no time at all he had the disgusting reptile in his hands and was carrying it off into the brush, depositing it a safe distance away. When he returned, Bernadette was on her knees, sucking air into her lungs with a vengeance.

'What happened?' he asked as he frowned down at her, hands on his hips.

She stared up at him in idiotic disbelief. 'What happened! What *happened*! That revolting thing leaped out of a tree at me and nearly crushed me to death, *that's* what *happened*!' she croaked.

Forrester heaved an exaggerated sigh as he squatted in front of her.

'Snakes are physiologically incapable of leaping, Sister. He must have fallen, and if you'd only kept your head, instead of scaring him half to death——'

'*I* scared *him!*' Bernadette echoed in a squawk.

'That's right. He'd fallen once, and he didn't want to repeat the experience, that's all. If you'd just calmly lowered yourself to the ground, instead of leaping about like a madwoman and shrieking at the top of your lungs, he'd have crawled off and gone his merry way, and no harm done.'

Bernadette gaped at him for a moment before she found her voice.

'Well how was I supposed to know that? Of *course* I yelled, for heaven's sake!' she finally defended. '*Anybody* would have yelled! Are you going to tell me that if a twenty-foot snake fell out of a tree on you, *you* wouldn't yell?'

He gave her a haughty, slightly disdainful look as he rose to his feet, and that was all the answer she got. Of course he wouldn't. She must be out of her feeble mind to even suggest he would.

'I hate snakes,' she muttered as he gave her a hand up. 'I've *always* hated snakes. My older brothers used to keep them as pets, in an old aquarium. Once two of them got out, and I woke up that night to find that they'd crawled under the covers with me.' She shuddered at the memory.

'Mmm, that must have been the root cause of this phobia you have about them.'

'I do not have a *phobia*,' Bernadette stated distinctly. 'I simply *hate . . . snakes*! They're ugly, and slimy, and——'

'They're not, you know. Slimy,' he argued in a maddeningly reasonable tone as she slipped back into her pack. 'Their skin is actually smooth, quite pleasant to touch.'

'I'll take your word for it,' Bernadette muttered. 'They're still disgusting creatures, and I hate, loathe, and despise them.'

She could have hit him for the amused gleam in his eye as he commented: 'I thought you—nuns, that is— were supposed to love all God's creatures, no matter how repulsive.'

Her lips compressing obstinately, Bernadette retorted: 'Serpents are the exception. It was a serpent, if you'll recall, that tempted Eve and thereby introduced original sin to the human race.'

He merely quirked one eyebrow at her and then headed off down the trail again, leaving Bernadette to stumble along behind, as usual. All afternoon her eyes kept darting overhead, but there were no more pythons lurking in the trees to ambush her. If she'd seen one draped along any of the branches Forrester passed under, she was gleefully considering tossing a stick at it. It would be interesting to see how he *really* reacted, the pompous ass!

By midafternoon the trees were growing noticeably

closer together, so that only rare glimpses of the sky could be seen. For most of the day they'd been passing through a belt that comprised part of the plantation area, where the forest had been thinned; but now Bernadette realised they must have left the last plantation behind, and with it, the last chance of human contact for God knew how many miles. If she could have summoned the energy, she'd have been angry. As it was, she had all she could do to keep her feet moving, taking one dragging step after another, not allowing herself to think beyond the next few yards.

'All right, this is as good a place as any.'

When Forrester stopped, she didn't even notice. Like an automaton, she trudged on, and only his light grasp on her arm finally halted her. She lifted a wan face in question, her eyes blank and glazed with fatigue.

'What?' she mumbled. 'I'm sorry, did you say something?'

He took in her utter exhaustion, the welts and splotches on her colourless face, and his gaze softened.

'I said we'll stop here for the night,' he said quietly.

Bernadette's 'Thank God!' was a fervent sigh as she let her head drop forward.

Without speaking, he removed her pack. Bernadette wasn't sure whether she sank to the ground all on her own, or if he helped her. Frankly, she didn't really care. Her ribcage felt ready to cave in, and every deep breath was agony. She tried to console herself with the thought that at least the pain in her sides took her mind off the pulsing ache in her head and the blisters on her feet.

Forrester's hands were impersonally gentle as they eased her on to her back, and she let her eyes droop closed. Oh, heaven, not to have to slog through muck and mire, fighting grasping vines and slapping branches every lousy step of the way. She dimly realised that he was unbuttoning her blouse, and then his hard, calloused palms were running over her tender sides. Bernadette flinched when he probed a particularly sensitive spot.

'That snake didn't do your ribs a lot of good,' he murmured. 'How's the head?'

'Compared to what?' she responded, attempting a smile and not quite carrying it off.'

'Lie still. I'll be back in a minute.'

Lie still, indeed. It would take a stampeding herd of elephants, at the very least, to move her from this spot.

When he returned, he ministered to her as carefully and competently as any nurse. Her skin knew the cool, soothing balm of a pungent ointment, and the stings miraculously stopped stinging. He popped some sort of pill into the back of her mouth, held a canteen to her lips so that she could swallow it, and within minutes she knew relief from aches and pains. He even peeled off her shoes and socks to see to the blisters.

'Give the medication a little while to take effect, then I'll bind your ribs,' he said, then moved away.

Bernadette's eyes opened at that, and she watched him warily as he gathered a couple of elastic bandages from the medical kit in her pack. But by the time he was ready, the potent painkiller–muscle relaxant he'd given her had done its job, and she wouldn't have uttered a word of protest if he'd stripped her naked and painted her passionate purple.

'There, you should be more comfortable now. Give me a few minutes, and I'll see what I can throw together for supper,' he said as he refastened her blouse.

'I'm not hungry,' Bernadette mumbled. 'Can't I please just go to sleep now?'

'As soon as you've eaten,' was his determined response.

But she must have dropped off, because when she next became aware of her surroundings he was gently nudging her shoulder and her salivary glands were responding to the distinct aroma of cooking meat.

'Sister Bernadette. Come on, I want you to eat something.'

In the moment or two before she remembered she was supposed to be a nun, she almost asked him why on earth he was calling her sister. Then fortunately her brain started functioning again, and she struggled to a sitting position. Forrester's hand curved under her arm to help.

'Take it easy. Feeling a bit more human?'

Bernadette looked up in surprise. He certainly *sounded* more human, and that in itself was enough to lift her spirits.

'Yes, thank you. How long did I sleep?'

He was on one knee beside her, so close that she could make out each bristle on his unshaven jaw. He propped an arm across his knee and astonished her by actually smiling—well, almost smiling, anyway, as close as he probably ever came.

'Almost two hours. It did you good, you needed the rest. Hungry?'

'Famished!' she admitted with such feeling that his almost-smile briefly became the genuine article.

'Good.' He rose to his feet and held out a hand. 'I decided a fire would be safe, so we've got real food tonight.'

The 'real food' turned out to be some kind of small animal which he'd roasted on a crude spit, and a root that tasted a lot like sweet potatoes. Bernadette hadn't exaggerated; she *was* famished, and neither of them spoke until their appetites had been appeased.

'Mmm, that was delicious,' she murmured as she licked meat grease from her fingers. 'Why wasn't it safe to have a fire before?'

Forrester's mouth slanted in amusement as he settled back, supporting himself on his elbows, one long leg bent at the knee. He still wore the pistol, and the rifle was lying near by, within easy reach.

'I was wondering when you'd get around to asking,' he drawled as he watched her pull on her shoes and socks. Apparently his temper improved when he had a full stomach; there wasn't a trace of sarcasm in his gravelly voice.

'I know I've pushed you pretty hard the last couple of days,' he said solemnly, 'but there were good reasons. The area where Claude was forced to set down isn't exactly the healthiest place in Africa at the moment. I take it you know something of the problems Prince Tzongari is having?'

Bernadette nodded. 'For centuries his family ruled a

small state which is now part of Southern Zaire and a small portion of Northern Zambia. I believe King Leopold II of Belgium first took control from the native rulers, sometime around 1885. Then in the latter 1890s, when the British began assuming control of Zambia and Rhodesia, he sectioned the state off and ceded a part of it as Zambian territory. With the emergence of so many new, independent African nations recently, Prince Tzongari decided to try and regain the control his ancestors had been stripped of. But from what I've heard, he's got a hard row to hoe, as we say back home.'

As Forrester listened, his face underwent a change. When she finished, his grave expression had been replaced by surprised respect.

'Very good, Sister,' he drawled. 'Are all nuns so well informed?'

Bernadette shrugged. 'I live here, Colonel, and Prince Tzongari's daughters are two of my students.'

'And I gather he's one of your several generous patrons.'

'Yes. As head of his family, he still controls several copper mines and one diamond mine, I believe.'

'Two,' Forrester corrected. 'As well as a small gold mine and part interest in a cotton plantation.'

Bernadette was impressed. 'I knew he was a wealthy man, but I never realised *how* wealthy.' A short, thoughtful silence elapsed, and then she murmured, 'So he could probably even afford to staff and equip his own army.'

'Can and has,' Forrester confirmed softly.

'And the cargo you were delivering——'

'Was intended for his men, yes.' He looked troubled. Not worried; she doubted he'd ever be uncertain enough about anything to be truly worried ... just faintly troubled.

'And now?' Bernadette asked. 'Did Claude go ahead and make his scheduled landing, even without you?'

Forrester shifted a little and shook his head. 'Too risky. There's no way of knowing who sabotaged the engines. No, he was going to change course for

Lubumbashi, refuel and make the necessary repairs, and then fly the girls and Mrs Alstadt straight home.'

'Althoff,' Bernadette corrected automatically, and his mouth tilted in wry amusement.

'Whatever.'

'You don't think one of the Prince's own men could have been responsible, do you? For the sabotage?'

'It's possible. Men have been known to commit far more traitorous acts, for the right price.'

But not this man, Bernadette thought as she gazed at him silently. His loyalty would never be up for sale, auctioned off to the highest bidder. He was hard, and he was tough and cynical, but an opportunist, he wasn't. Whatever course he set himself on, for whatever reasons, he would alter it only when *he* decided to do so, and then he would explain or excuse himself to no one.

As the silence stretched out he sat up to take a slim metal case from his shirt pocket and extracted a cheroot. Bernadette watched his lean, competent fingers as he struck a match and lit the slender cigar, and wondered with a morbid curiosity how many lives he'd taken. What a thought! But she couldn't dismiss or deny it, just as she knew she would never ask.

He was a paradox, she decided, watching the blue smoke swirl around his head. Those hands, which she had no doubt could be cruel and absolutely ruthless at times, could also be as gentle and caring as any mother's. Hadn't she known their gentleness only a couple of hours before? Then, too, this man, who she instinctively knew did not make a habit of explaining his actions, had made a point of telling her why he'd pushed them both so hard the last two days. For the first time, he hadn't been mocking or patronising or arrogant; he'd addressed her as an equal, a mature adult who had the right to know what the situation was and the intelligence to understand it. Yet she had it on good authority that he held most women in low regard, if not outright contempt. A paradox, she thought again.

'You're unusually quiet,' drawled the object of her thoughts.

'I was just thinking.'

'Not praying? Don't you have a quota or something?'

Bernadette decided he wasn't being snide, only teasing. She was beginning to learn to tell the difference.

'I met my quota for the next week, while I was waiting for you to get around to peeling that snake off me,' she responded drily.

His laughter was yet one more surprise. Low and rich, it was lovely to hear—totally masculine, like the rest of him, yet at the same time oddly melodious and totally unselfconscious.

'I like that,' she said softly. 'You should laugh more often.'

He gave her an odd look, like she'd said something surprising, then shrugged. 'So should you. I heard you laughing with Claude the other night. It sounded like music . . . bells. You laughed easily, like you do it a lot.'

Bernadette was momentarily taken aback. The observation was so unexpected, so unlike his usual gruff cynicism, that she was at a loss as to how to respond.

'I do. That is . . .' she smiled sheepishly, 'usually, I do. When I'm not worried sick about how I'm going to get six students and their ailing headmistress home, or trying to contend with a surly jungle commando, or fighting off swarms of bloodthirsty insects.'

Forrester grinned in appreciation, his strong teeth gleaming in the firelight. 'Well, you can take it from the jungle commando, Sister, you're not doing half bad so far.'

Bernadette merely inclined her head in gracious acknowledgement of the compliment.

'Besides the brothers who collected snakes, have you got any other family?'

'Oh, yes,' she said with a fond smile. 'Altogether there are four boys and two girls, our parents, and one grandmother. Plus lots of cousins and aunts and uncles. How about you?'

He shook his head, making the cigar glow red as he pulled hard at it. 'I was an only child, and both my parents have been dead for some time.'

Something in his voice, an indefinable something she couldn't quite hook on to, made Bernadette refrain from questioning him further, though she'd have liked to know more. She contented herself with a trite but sincere, 'I'm sorry.'

'As I said, they've been gone a long time,' Forrester murmured around the cheroot. The words and the tone in which he spoke them were dismissive, but Bernadette didn't miss the tension in his long, hard body.

Suddenly their eyes met and held, and Bernadette experienced the most incredible feelings. She wanted to go to his side, put her arms around him, console him for losses she could sense he had suffered, hold him, comfort him. It was ridiculous, she realised that. Of all the people she'd ever known, Sam Forrester would be the last to need consoling or comforting, and the first to reject any attempt to do either. He was totally self-sufficient, complete within himself. And why on earth should that make her feel sad?

There was a loud popping noise from the fire, and she jerked out of her strange, reflective mood with a self-conscious laugh. Forrester's gaze was indulgently amused as he continued to watch her.

'Tell me, Sister, what makes a woman like you decide to become a nun?' he asked lazily. 'An unhappy love affair?'

'Sorry to disappoint you, Colonel, but I've never had a love affair, unhappy or otherwise,' she replied lightly.

Which was true enough, though the fact had nothing to do with a vow of chastity. She just hadn't ever met a man who affected her strongly enough, physically. A few of her friends—and most of the men she'd dated—had tried to convince her she was abnormal, even frigid. Bernadette knew better. What she was was choosy; discriminating; fastidious, even. But definitely not frigid.

'I can't relate to people like you,' Forrester claimed with a puzzled shake of his head.

'People who practice celibacy, you mean?' Bernadette asked drily. 'Sex isn't like air, Colonel. You don't expire if you do without it.'

'I wouldn't know,' he murmured, the suggestion of a smile showing around the cheroot as he stuck it back in his mouth.

'I'm living proof.'

The cheroot stayed between his teeth as he stretched out on his side, facing her, one hand supporting his head. 'If you say so.'

Bernadette gazed at him steadily. He was goading her, trying to provoke her into losing her temper. She knew it and refused to be provoked.

'Okay, that was a cheap shot,' he muttered when the silence had become impossible to ignore. He removed the cheroot and studied the tip with a slight frown. 'With you, it's believable. But I have trouble accepting the idea that all nuns, and especially priests, actually live entirely celibate lives.'

'Why especially priests?' Bernadette asked. His mocking, smugly masculine glance did what his taunt had failed to do, and she found herself challenging him.

'You surely don't cling to the ridiculous belief that men have stronger sex drives than women? In this day and age, a man of your experience? Or hasn't the sexual revolution caught up with you yet?'

His eyes narrowed against the cigar smoke as he exhaled slowly. 'You seem to know a lot about the game, for someone who claims never to have been a player,' he mocked.

Bernadette refused to back down. 'They don't perform lobotomies on novice nuns, Colonel,' she retorted crisply,

'Meaning you experience all the baser desires of the flesh, I gather?'

His harsh voice was softly insinuating, making her suddenly uncomfortable. Good Lord, how had they progressed to such an intimate conversation?

'Of course,' she said in an unexpectedly husky voice. 'I'm not a machine, or some kind of freak.'

'And what do you do, when you have those ... feelings?' he probed softly.

'Pray.'

The answer was subdued, but fervent, and her eyes shied away from his intent, direct stare.

Forrester made a sound halfway between a grunt and a snort of disbelief, but thankfully didn't pursue the matter. Bernadette had just started to relax when he spoke again.

'Where are your ring and your rosary?'

She floundered for a moment, then said the first thing that came to mind.

'I didn't think it would be wise to wander the streets of Mombasa wearing a gold ring, so I put it in my bag, with——'

'The rosary. And then left the bag on the plane,' he finished for her. His tone implied that such a lapse was only to be expected from a mere female.

'That's right,' Bernadette murmured meekly, stifling her irritation at his chauvinism.

'Don't you feel . . . naked, without them?'

He was serious, she realised just in time to stop a sharp retort. Her mouth curved slightly as she shook her head.

'No more naked than you must feel when you aren't wearing a gun, Colonel,' she said quietly. 'To be honest, I do wish I had the bag, though. Then I could at least comb my hair.'

'Vanity, thy name is woman,' he drawled.

'It isn't vain to want to be clean and well groomed. Are we going to Lubumbashi, too?' she asked hastily, to take his mind off anything more personal.

'That's the plan.'

Bernadette's frown was pensive. 'How long do you estimate it will take to get there?'

He gnawed on the cheroot as he considered. 'We're nearly three hundred kilometres from there, now. Provided we don't run into any problems, we should make it in another five days or so.'

'Three hundred kilometres!'

It came out an awed whisper. She did some rapid calculation, and came up with the daunting figure of over thirty miles a day. Why not? she thought with a touch of hysteria. Marathon runners covered twenty-six miles in something over two hours, didn't they? But through jungle and swamps? And they only had to worry about the occasional dog nipping at their heels; here, if anything tried to take a hunk out of you, it for sure wouldn't be some old lady's cocker spaniel.

'What kind of "problems" were you thinking of?' she asked, not at all sure she wanted to know.

Forrester shrugged indifferently. 'The usual thing—animal attacks, snake bite, rivers too swollen to cross. And then of course we'll have to be on the alert for unfriendly natives and any traps or pits they might have left. Fortunately there's been no sign of the government troops opposing Tzongari's men, at least so far.'

'Thank God for small favours,' Bernadette muttered to herself.

Forrester grunted agreement. 'Amen to that, Sister. As far as they're concerned, I'm an enemy agent, and since you're with me . . .' He trailed off with another shrug. 'I don't need to tell you how unpleasant being captured would be, especially if they happened to find the cargo we left back there.'

No, he certainly didn't need to tell her, Bernadette thought with a gulp. He'd said more than enough, already.

'You ought to turn in,' he remarked after a minute. 'You're exhausted, and we've still got a lot of ground to cover.'

Bernadette followed the suggestion willingly, but her eyes didn't close until after he'd returned from carrying their food scraps a good distance into the brush. He didn't immediately lie down on his own sleeping bag—she'd noticed last night that he didn't confine himself by getting inside it—but sat beside the fire to clean and oil both his weapons. She supposed that would be necessary because of the high humidity. Then again, maybe he was just a creature of habit, or wanted something to occupy him while he stood watch.

The man was an enigma, she thought drowsily as her eyelids drooped: one minute an impossible tyrant, the next reasonable, even considerate. She couldn't figure him out, and it would probably be useless to try. But one thing she did know, and couldn't afford to forget. He was not only shrewd and clever as the very devil, but too observant by far.

Five more days, she told herself grimly. For her own protection, she had to act, speak, even *think* like a nun for five more days. *Oh Lord, give me strength*, was her heartfelt prayer as she sank into a heavy, dreamless sleep.

CHAPTER FIVE

THEY were on the move again early the next morning. Bernadette was stiff and sore in every muscle and her joints ached from sleeping on the hard ground, but her head and ribs felt immeasurably better, thanks to Forrester's care the night before. He seemed to be in a more relaxed mood this morning, as well. Halfway through the morning he stopped and waited for her to catch up to him, observing her through narrowed eyes as she approached.

'How are you doing?'

Bernadette smiled. 'I'm fine.'

He examined her face closely as he shook a cigarette out of a half-empty pack and lit it, then nodded, apparently satisfied with what he saw.

'You shouldn't smoke so much,' she told him quietly.

His mouth quirked in what she had come to think of as his quasi-grin. 'You worry about my immortal soul, Sister, and leave the container to me, hmm?'

Bernadette gave him another smile, not at all put out by his mockery. 'If you insist,' she replied, then added matter-of-factly, 'It's just that it's such a superbly constructed container, and I hate to see you abuse it, Colonel.'

She turned and walked off in the direction they'd been going, but not before she saw his eyes narrow in surprise. Her mouth twitched when he growled:

'That's a hell of a thing for a nun to say!'

'Why?' Bernadette answered calmly. 'I do have eyes in my head, and an appreciation for beauty in all its forms.'

'Including the male body?' Forrester demanded, sounding faintly shocked.

Bernadette kept walking, not looking back. She was afraid she might grin if she saw the expression on his face.

'The Bible tells us that God created man in His own

image,' she pointed out, adding: *And He certainly outdid Himself on you, Sugar*, silently, to herself.

He muttered something under his breath as he started after her, and it was all Bernadette could do to keep the amusement out of her voice as she asked: 'What was that, Colonel?'

'I said, you're the damnedest female I've ever met,' he growled. 'And outspoken as hell, for a nun. I thought you were supposed to practice meekness, make a virtue of humility. My God, some of the things that come out of your mouth!'

Bernadette grasped a tangle of vines blocking her path and ripped a hole to pass through, and didn't respond.

'You've never once told me not to swear. Not *once*!' He made it an accusation as he reached around her to hold the vines out of the way. His arm brushed against hers, his skin warm and firm.

'Would it have done any good?' Bernadette countered.

'That's not the bloody point! Nuns are supposed to be—I don't know . . . hell, you're supposed to be like our consciences.'

'Don't you already possess a conscience? You know when you've committed a wrong, don't you, without someone else pointing it out?'

'Oh, Christ!' Forrester muttered in exasperation.

'And would my constantly nagging at you about your language cause you to suddenly start talking like a Sunday School teacher?'

'Not bloody likely!'

'Well, then. Why should I frustrate myself and irritate you, over something we both know isn't going to change?'

She was frankly enjoying the sparring, the verbal give and take. Her face was animated, her eyes sparkling, as she stepped clear of the twisted maze of vines and came face to face with four of the most awesome ugly men she'd ever seen in her life. When she froze to the spot in shock, Forrester came up against her back with a gentle bump.

'Easy,' he murmured in her ear. His hands grasped her shoulders briefly, and then one arm dropped to encircle her waist and pull her back against him as he said something to the men in what Bernadette supposed was some obscure African dialect.

She didn't speak out against his precipitate embrace, or the unmistakable possessiveness in it. She understood at once that it was for the others' benefit, and stood quietly, submissively, glad for his solid strength at her back.

They weren't much taller than her, but each of them was adorned—faces and bodies—in the most outlandish fashion, like a collage of all the pictures she'd ever seen in *National Geographic*. Decorative scars, punctured ears, lips and nostrils studded with gold, loincloths, shields and primitive spears—these four men, all by themselves, formed a composite of everything she'd imagined Africa to be, since childhood.

But on closer inspection, they weren't really ugly. Not at all; just something totally new to her experience.

One—she supposed the leader—responded to Forrester's greeting, and then there was a brief exchange. His arm tightened around her. In warning, or reassurance? Bernadette turned her face up to him, and was the recipient of a smile so warm and tender it rendered her speechless. She'd never have believed that hard, cynical mouth could be capable of such a smile.

'It's all right, darling, they're friends,' he said softly.

Darling! Her expression must have conveyed her shock, because his fingers suddenly dug into her midriff, and this time she had no doubt she was being given a warning.

'O-oh!' she stammered.

'I've explained that it's your first trip into the bush, and that you're just a bit jumpy.' He was still smiling, and Bernadette was still in a mild state of shock, but not so much that she didn't recognise the wary, on-guard look in his eyes and the tension in his body.

'Yes. Yes, that's right!' She flashed a nervous smile, first at Forrester and then at the four expressionless men. 'Just a little. Do these, er ... gentlemen, speak English?'

A pleased look entered his eyes and his grip relaxed. 'Unfortunately, they tell me they don't. They've invited us back to their village. It would be an insult to refuse.'

'Well ... we certainly wouldn't want to insult them, would we?' Bernadette murmured as she eyed their spears.

'My sentiments exactly,' was Forrester's dry response as he smilingly indicated that their hosts should lead the way.

'They're Bantu,' he managed to tell her as they dropped a little behind. 'Probably harmless, to us, but keep your eyes and ears open, and follow my lead.'

'What did you tell them?' Bernadette whispered. 'About me—what I'm doing with you?'

'That you're my woman, and that I had to shoot a rich French trader in Manono to get you.'

'What!' It was a horrified squeak.

'Keep your voice down, for God's sake!' he growled softly. 'If they think you belong to me, that I'll fight to keep you for myself, they'll probably keep their hands off.'

'Only "probably"?' she asked in a strangled voice.

'Don't worry, Sister,' Forrester drawled. 'If anybody touches you once we get to their village, it'll be yours truly. And whatever I do or say, you go along. Got it?'

His voice was totally devoid of humour; it was as flinty hard as his eyes. Bernadette gulped and nodded.

'Got it,' she breathed. 'You think they do speak English, in spite of what they said, don't you?'

'They may not speak it, but there are damned few Bantu left who don't understand at least a few words. Just to be on the safe side, don't say any more than you have to.'

Bernadette considered being insulted, then decided it was probably good advice and merely nodded again.

'And don't be afraid,' he added quietly. 'I'll take care of you.'

'I know you will. I'm not afraid,' Bernadette said just as quietly.

Forrester shot her a keen look, then unexpectedly grinned. 'Good girl.'

Strangely, the lopsided grin and two carelessly spoken words did more to relieve her anxiety than anything else would have.

As it turned out, there didn't appear to be anything to be afraid *of*. They were greeted like visiting royalty and entertained with music and dancing until long after dark.

It had taken about three hours to reach the small collection of thatched huts, and by the time they arrived Bernadette was more than ready for the soupy bowl of cooked, mashed roots mixed with grain that was put before her. She didn't even mind the lack of utensils, digging in with a hunk of unleavened bread and her fingers, and Emily Post be damned. When she caught Forrester's amused glance, she shrugged and belatedly crossed herself, and his rich laughter brought a flush to her cheeks.

That had been a stupid slip-up. Until now, she'd always remembered to give grave thanks for her food, even if it was only beef sticks eaten on the trail. But he'd apparently put her lapse down to acute hunger and nerves, because other than laughing at her, he made no comment.

After they'd eaten, he drew her aside, an arm draped casually over her shoulders.

'I'll be spending some time with the men, now. It's expected. Stay with the women. They'll fuss over you and giggle a lot and chatter like a bunch of magpies. but don't worry about not understanding a word they say. Just smile and nod, and they'll be happy. And whatever you do, for God's sake don't let any of them get a hand on your gun.'

Bernadette gazed up at him uncertainly. She was acutely aware of his proximity, the fact that her breast was brushing his chest and they were standing hip to hip. But what upset her was the fact that he was going to leave her alone with a bunch of—as far as she could tell—savages. She suddenly wanted to cling to him, to beg him not to go. But of course she didn't.

'How long——?' she began nervously.

'Just a few hours, until the evening meal. Don't look

so panic-stricken, it'll be all right.' His voice was gruff
with impatience, but he took time to give her shoulders
a brief squeeze before relinquishing her to the waiting
women.

The rest of the afternoon passed quickly, and it was
an experience Bernadette knew she would never forget.
The women fussed over her just as Forrester had
predicted, bringing their children and even their animals
to her, showing them off with shy pride. When he came
to collect her, he found her seated on the earth floor of
one of the huts, feeding a baby goat milk from a
perforated leather pouch. She looked up as his tall form
filled the door and blocked out the light. She was
laughing, her eyes shining and her cheeks rosily flushed.
He went very still for an extended moment, and then his
voice, laced with sardonic amusement, intruded upon
the scene and sent the smaller children scurrying for the
safety of their mothers' arms.

'How rustic. Farmer Brown's daughter, I presume?'

'Actually, no.' Bernadette laughed as the goat bleated
and rooted for its makeshift nipple. 'It's Judge
Chapman's daughter, and he'd probably fall over
laughing if he could see her now.'

'Sounds like a man after my own heart. I thought
you might be ready for a break, but if you'd rather stay
and feed the livestock——'

'I'm coming!' she said quickly, before he could go
away again. She handed the kid over to one of the
women and scrambled to her feet, brushing the dust
from her jeans.

'Phew! I smell like goat!'

Forrester's lips twitched as he observed her. 'Being a
gentleman of sorts, I won't comment,' he drawled as he
accepted her pack from another of the women. 'But
don't fret over it. I doubt anyone here will notice.
Would you like to see the rest of the village before
supper?'

'I'd love to!' Bernadette answered eagerly. 'Would it
be all right? They won't mind us wandering around on
our own?'

'If they do, I imagine they'll stop us,' was his lazy

response as he followed her outside. For a moment the answer gave Bernadette pause, and then she sensed that he was teasing and relaxed.

By the time they'd made a circuit of the rest of the village, people had begun to gather around a communal cooking fire.

'And how did you pass the afternoon, Colonel?' Bernadette asked as they started back at a leisurely pace.

'Hunting lion.'

The matter-of-fact response brought her to an abrupt halt, her eyes widening as she stared up at his rugged face.

'Oh. Well, did you find any?' she asked humorously, falling in beside him again.

'Just the one. When it's time to eat, they'll expect you to serve me. Just watch the other women and do what they do. I imagine it'll be all right if you sit beside me, since we're both guests.'

'I'm honoured,' Bernadette muttered under her breath. She gave him a frowning glance, but his expressionless features told her nothing. Was he putting her on about going on a lion hunt? She wouldn't give him the satisfaction of asking, but with him, anything was possible. Anything at all.

After she'd dutifully served him, Bernadette followed the example set by the other women and helped herself to a significantly smaller portion, then took her place on the ground at his side. This time she remembered to give quiet thanks for the food and ask God's blessing on the hosts who had provided it.

'Mmm, good,' she murmured as she munched on a stick of crunchy something-or-other. 'What is it, do you know?'

Forrester waited until she'd swallowed and daintily tucked a piece of meat into her mouth, then answered, 'Fried blood,' in a laconic drawl.

She stopped chewing and looked at him with a comical expression of dismay.

'What . . . kind?'

'Lion. Female. She'd been killing their livestock. The men who took part in the hunt have the option of drinking her blood and/or partaking of her heart. Gives them her strength and courage, or so they believe.'

The men who took part in the hunt. Determined not to gag, Bernadette shifted what was in her mouth to one side in case she decided to spit it out, and whispered:

'And this meat we're eating . . . is it——?'

'Oh, no, this isn't lion,' Forrester assured her, and Bernadette swallowed in relief. 'Tastes more like dog, actually.'

She choked, and he quickly held a wooden cup to her lips. Bernadette recoiled from it violently.

'Goat's milk!' he muttered. 'Goat's milk, I swear. That's all. For God's sake, don't be sick. They'd all be offended.'

Bernadette nodded and gratefully gulped down the milk, then breathed deeply through her mouth for several minutes.

'Don't tell me you've never eaten dog,' Forrester drawled as he returned his attention to his meal.

Bernadette felt like emptying her bowl in his lap, but limited herself to giving him a fierce look which he completely ignored.

'Oh, sure,' she muttered in a voice pitched for his ears alone. 'My mother used to serve it every Tuesday, with broccoli and potatoes au gratin. We usually had apple pie for dessert.'

He tried and failed to control a grin, which infuriated her.

'You sick, demented man,' she hissed. 'You really enjoyed doing that to me, didn't you?'

Forrester shook his head in denial. 'No. Of course not.' The tremor of laughter in his voice caused her fists to clench as she fought to control her temper.

'Liar!' she snapped. 'You *liar*! You *did* enjoy it!'

His hateful amusement found release in a throaty chuckle, enraging her and robbing her of the power of speech.

'You're right,' he admitted, then laughed again, obviously enjoying himself tremendously at her expense. 'Just the look on your face!' He risked a glance at said face, and what he saw there wiped the grin right off his mouth, though his eyes still glittered wickedly.

'I'm sorry, Sister,' he murmured with a ludicrous attempt at humility. 'Truly. I don't know what got into me. I promise, I'll let you finish your meal in peace.'

As if she'd be able to swallow another bite! Hours later, after the food and dishes had been cleared away and the primitive beat of native drums and reed wind instruments was pounding in her veins, Bernadette sat still and silent, intensely aware of the man at her side.

After her anger had cooled, she'd begun to see the humour in the situation, and wonder at the imp of mischief in him that had provoked such behaviour. It seemed a contradiction in terms to think of Sam Forrester as being playful, but in his offbeat way, that was exactly what he had been. Not cruel, or even malicious; just playful. The realisation both surprised and puzzled her, and she couldn't help wondering how many more facets there were to his complex personality.

When the dancing finally ended, the celebrations for the successful hunt at an end, everyone began sidling off in twos and threes. Bernadette didn't speak as Forrester led the way to where their sleeping bags had been spread. She stopped at his side, staring down at them, feeling a strange tautening in the pit of her stomach.

'And just whose idea, pray tell, was this?' she said very softly.

Someone had zipped the two bags together to form one king-sized bedroll.

'Don't look at me,' Forrester drawled. 'The women must have done it. They *would* assume we'd want it this way.'

'Well, they *would* be mistaken. Separate them, please.' She was suddenly nervous, on edge. She couldn't sleep inside the double bag with him, he must realise that.

'That wouldn't be wise,' he murmured. 'There are several pairs of eyes watching us at this moment, and if it appears we aren't as close as I've led them to believe, some of those men might be tempted to come out and offer themselves in my place.'

Bernadette closed her eyes, then released a long,

resigned breath. 'All right, you've made your point.'

'Of course, if you insist . . .' Forrester taunted lazily.

'All *right*, I said!'

A few minutes later, after a hasty trip behind the nearest hut, she removed her gunbelt and shoes and squirmed into the bag. He, of course, was already occupying half of it. More than half, actually.

'Don't let me interrupt your evening prayers,' he murmured.

Oh, no! She'd completely forgotten. 'I won't,' she murmured, finding that it was literally impossible to prevent their bodies from making contact within the confines of the bag. 'Good night, Colonel.'

'Just pretend I'm not here. I won't make a sound.'

'I appreciate your consideration,' Bernadette murmured, wishing she had the nerve to slap his mocking face. 'I'll try not to disturb you.'

'Oh, you won't. Not a bit. Go right ahead. I'll just lie here and keep still. I won't even listen.'

Bernadette wanted to scream. At the top of her lungs. Instead, she closed her eyes and began to murmur softly (and she hoped unintelligibly) under her breath—nursery rhymes, a couple of stanzas from *The Village Blacksmith*, and just to round things out, a few lines from Dan Fogelberg's 'Leader of the Band'. She kept her voice in a monotone, the words evenly spaced, as if she'd done it all a thousand times and knew the whole rigamarole by heart. When she finished, she awkwardly crossed herself and released a heavy sigh.

'All done?'

She groaned inwardly and murmured a subdued, 'Yes.'

'That didn't take long. Must have been the condensed version,' Forrester mocked.

Before she could respond, he had rolled to his side and was leaning over her, one arm across her body.

'Colonel!' Bernadette said sharply. It had been a long day, and she really didn't feel like ending it with a wrestling match.

'Shh. They're still watching. I want them to at least *think* there's something happening out here besides your now-I-lay-me-down-to-sleep routine.'

His harsh voice was loaded with cynical amusement, and Bernadette glared up at him, her eyes glittering angrily in the darkness.

'You can be really despicable when you set your mind to it,' she said quietly.

'And now you'll have to say another prayer, to ask forgiveness for what you're thinking about me,' he taunted, his voice a soft growl.

'I'd be awake all night,' she retorted in a fair imitation of his drawl. 'You're about to suffocate me, or was that the idea?' He *was* close—much too close, and much too big, and much, much too good looking, damn him.

He didn't answer, his lips curving in a wolfish grin as he drew her up against him, shifting his weight to hold her in a close but undemanding embrace.

'You are the damnedest woman,' he murmured, sounding both surprised and amused. 'You'd make one hell of a soldier, do you know that, Sister?'

'I can't quite picture myself marching into battle,' Bernadette replied drily. The words came out a little stilted. The situation wasn't exactly conducive to remaining loose and relaxed; she was too aware of the lean, hard length of his body pressing against the softer lines of hers.

'No? I seem to recall another lady of a religious bent doing just that. Joan, her name was, Joan of Orleans. I think she must have been a lot like you,' he said softly, his warm breath fanning her cheek.

'You flatter me, Colonel.' Bernadette's voice was decidedly husky, and she was suddenly having trouble regulating her breathing. It was showing an alarming tendency to catch and shudder in her throat.

'Sam,' he murmured. 'I've told you before, I'm not any kind of colonel any more.'

She swallowed nervously, trying to work up some saliva. What was he doing? He surely didn't have it in mind to seduce a *nun*, did he? Lord, she hoped not, because she had the sinking feeling that it might not be all that difficult, and then where would she be? Several hundred miles from nowhere, with a guilt-ridden male who had already done his worst and had nothing to lose by continuing what he'd started, *that* was where! She stirred uneasily under his penetrating, narrow-eyed gaze, and was immediately sorry when the slight movement brought her breasts into closer contact with the solid wall of his chest. She desperately hoped he couldn't detect the immediate hardening of her nipples through their clothes.

'Do you know what I'm wondering?' he asked softly when she didn't speak. Bernadette shook her head stiffly. 'You said when you have those feelings, about a man, that you pray until they pass. I'm wondering ... in your case, just how often does that kind of prayer become necessary, Sister?'

Bernadette felt guilty heat suffuse her. Her mouth went as dry as dust, and her toes curled inside her socks. 'Not often,' she answered in a tight little voice.

Forrester's mouth tilted in derision. 'And I always thought nuns didn't lie. Tell me, Sister, just out of curiosity ... are you praying, now?'

She closed her eyes, her body held rigidly still. 'As hard as I can,' she said impulsively, and as it happened, honestly.

She felt him tense against her. He stayed where he was, silent and motionless save for the steady rise and fall of his chest, for an eternal sixty seconds. And then he abruptly released her and rolled on to his back.

'Say one for me, while you're at it,' he muttered harshly.

CHAPTER SIX

THEY took their leave of the Bantu early the next morning. It was their fourth day on the trail, and according to Forrester's calculations they still had three to go before they reached Lubumbashi, near the Zambian border.

Bernadette was pleased to discover as the morning wore on that the stiffness in her joints disappeared, her muscles were responding with very little complaint, and the tenderness around her ribcage was all but gone. She always tried to keep fit—exercising morning and night, riding her bicycle instead of driving, joining the students in volleyball and soccer games—and now it all seemed to be paying off. She didn't delude herself that she matched Forrester's superb conditioning, but at least she wouldn't slow him down.

She watched his broad back as he walked ahead of her, and frowned. He'd been a real bear this morning, his disposition rotten, his conversation—what there was of it—curt and limited to necessary instructions. It didn't take a genius to figure out that his attitude was caused by that little scene inside the sleeping bag last night, but she was at a loss to gauge his underlying mood.

What was he thinking, feeling? Obviously regret, for one thing, but what else? Surely not remorse, or guilt— she had a hard time accepting either possibility, though that was probably unfair of her. After all, he *did* believe she was a nun. Still, she had the nagging feeling that his abruptness, the way his mouth tightened whenever he looked back to make sure she was still with him, went deeper than a mild case of the guilts. The man was just too complicated for her to understand, she thought with a sigh. So why did she keep beating her head against the wall trying?

They halted early for lunch, and Bernadette didn't attempt to hide her surprise.

'We should be out of the danger area,' Forrester explained brusquely as he dropped his pack on the ground. 'We'll be able to take it a little easier from here on. Why don't you see if you can find some deadwood, and I'll make a fire.'

A fire! In the middle of the day! She didn't realise she'd spoken aloud until he turned towards her with a wry twist of his mouth.

'There's a small tributary of the Southern Congo just through those trees, over there,' he said, inclining his head. 'I thought you might appreciate a bath, and the chance to wash your clothes.'

Bernadette gaped at him a moment, then quickly shed her own pack and hurried off with an excited, 'I'll be right back with the wood.'

'Watch out for leaping snakes!' Forrester called after her, but she didn't dignify the remark by responding.

While she gathered as much wood as she could carry, it occurred to her to marvel that he was so familiar with the country he'd been able to come directly to where there was fresh water for bathing and doing laundry. How many other men could have done the same—at least, how many other White men? Not many, she'd be willing to bet.

'Is that enough?' she asked as she staggered back to where he was kneeling beside his pack and dumped her load of wood on the ground.

Forrester looked at the wood, then ran a hand over his stubbled cheek and across his mouth.

'Depends. Were you planning to put up a log cabin?'

'I got too much.' Bernadette shrugged. 'Oh, well, too much is better than not enough, right?'

Forrester glanced up at her, his dark brows lifting slightly. 'When it comes to firewood—definitely.' His expression was solemn, but there was an indefinable something in his deep voice that made Bernadette feel flushed. As she gazed at him in confusion, his mouth thinned and he abruptly turned away.

'Let me get the fire going, then I'll take you down to the river,' he said briskly.

He went ahead, holding vegetation aside as he led her

to the gently sloping bank of what looked more like a sluggish stream than a tributary of the mighty Congo.

'The water's not all that clean, but at least it's wet,' he drawled.

'I don't mind,' Bernadette assured him. 'I just wish I had some soap.'

He withdrew a small, hard-milled bar from his shirt pocket and handed it to her, and she smiled her gratitude.

'I don't need to warn you not to swallow any of the water, do I?'

Bernadette's lips curved in wry response. 'No.'

'Good. I doubt there's anything in there but a few fish—it's too shallow. But just to be safe, don't dawdle, and keep one eye peeled. I'll be just on the other side of those trees. And if you're the type who bursts into song in your bath, don't ... unless you wouldn't mind having me join you.'

'In other words, yell if I need you?' Bernadette murmured drily.

'You've got it, Sister.' He started back the way they'd come, then abruptly halted. His shoulders squared, as if he was bracing himself for something, and then he slowly turned to face her again. His face was a blankly beautiful mask, his eyes unrevealing.

'About last night,' he began.

Bernadette hurried to stop him. 'We don't have to discuss it, Colonel,' she said, her voice low.

'I have no intention of discussing it, Sister,' he growled. 'I just want you to know that you needn't be afraid. That is ... I won't deny that, being a normal, red-blooded male, I might occasionally feel a regrettable and possibly even immoral attraction to you. But I assure you there's no need to worry on that score. You're perfectly safe.'

Bernadette stared at him mutely, for once at a loss for words. Whew! He certainly believed in laying it on the line! Eventually she recovered enough to respond to his surprising but somehow touching reassurance.

'I knew that, Colonel,' she told him softly and sincerely. 'Whatever else you might be, you are a man of honour.' He gave a curt, stiff nod, but his gaze softened a little, encouraging her to add: 'And I don't believe any natural, instinctive human ... reaction ... could be considered immoral. Maybe I'm wrong, maybe——' She faltered, embarrassed, and yet compelled to be as forthright as he had been. 'No, I take that back. I'm not wrong,' she said with a defiant lift of her chin.

He didn't respond directly, just looked at her, an odd expression in his grey eyes. Then his mouth quirked in that crooked grin and he slowly shook his head.

'The damnedest woman,' he said softly, almost to himself. Then he seemed to give a mental shrug and gestured impatiently towards the water. 'Shake a leg, Sister. I'd like a bath, too, and we haven't got all day to waste.'

But as he started away for the second time, her distressed, 'Oh, no!' halted him.

'What?' He was beside her again at once. 'Did you spot something in the water?'

Bernadette shook her head with a frown. 'No. I just remembered—if I wash out my clothes, I don't have anything to wear while they dry.'

Forrester snapped his fingers in irritation. 'Damn! I've got an extra shirt in my pack I meant to bring. Hold on a minute, and I'll fetch it.'

Bernadette could tell just by looking at it that the shirt would be more like a burnoose on her—a voluminous, shapeless, dun-coloured tent. Which was probably just as well, she thought as she stepped out of her plain white cotton panties and into the water: the baggier, the better.

She hurried through washing and rinsing her hair, then lathered her body from head to toe. The soap, though it made her smell like a pair of cowboy boots, produced gobs of thick, rich suds. Before long the water downstream began to resemble a bubble bath.

Something brushed her foot, and she jumped in alarm. Fortunately, before she could decide to scream for Forrester she realised it was only a fish. And since piranha weren't indigenous to Africa, presumably a harmless species. A moment later she dissolved into helpless giggles.

'Was that a cry for help?' Forrester's amused voice drawled from beyond the trees.

'*No!* Stay there!' Bernadette ordered, then gurgled with laughter again. 'A fish is nibbling on my big toe.'

Had he really muttered, 'Lucky fish'? No, she must be hearing things.

'I'm almost finished. I'll be out in a minute.'

Enveloped in his shirt from chin to knees, she hastily rinsed out her clothes, using the soap on her shirt and underthings, then wrung them as dry as she could and carried them to where he waited, lounging against a tree with one of his cheroots sticking out of his mouth.

His eyes partially concealed by drooping lids, he subjected her to a slow scrutiny. Even without a mirror she knew what he was seeing: a slight girl whose unspectacular curves were concealed by the shirt, her short, wet hair a gleaming helmet above a face dominated by large violet eyes, her shapely calves and slender ankles looking even more pale than usual against the background of deep forest greens and browns. She held out the soap and he took it wordlessly.

'Your turn,' Bernadette said with an impulsive grin.

Forrester's lips parted in an answering smile, baring strong white teeth which were still clamped on the cheroot.

'You look like a lost little waif.'

'Please,' Bernadette protested with a pained expression. 'I'm nearly twenty-five years old, which surely disqualifies me as a waif, by anyone's standards.'

He didn't answer, but he was still smiling as he pushed off from the tree and headed for the river.

Bernadette replaced the rolled bandages in the medical kit and hung her clothes over branches and vines near the meagre fire, then decided to see what she could throw together in the way of a meal. It was high time she did some of the work, and besides, it might help keep her mind off Forrester, skinny-dipping less than thirty feet away. From what she'd already seen of his body, when he helped Claude clear the plane's fuel lines, she knew he'd be magnificent nude. She could imagine the smooth, rippling flex of muscles as he washed, the way the water would sheet over his skin, leaving it slick and glistening. When she realised that her hands were clenched into fists and she was breathing shallowly through her mouth, she gave herself a mental kick and knelt to yank open her pack.

By the time he returned she had lunch ready: canned chicken and peas, warmed in the skillet from his mess kit. She tried to keep her eyes from straying to his bare torso when he hung his wet shirt over a branch and joined her on the ground. *You're supposed to be a nun, for God's sake!* she reminded herself fiercely.

'Your clothes are going to smell like wood smoke,' he commented drily, accepting the tin plate she handed him. Their beverage was the usual water from a shared canteen.

Bernadette glanced up at the rapidly drying garments. 'It doesn't matter. We're starting to run low on water. Would it be safe to boil some from the river?'

'Safe, yes. But you wouldn't be able to tolerate either the smell or the taste. We're okay. We'll have fresh water tomorrow.'

'We will?' She shifted to face him, her gaze eagerly questioning. 'Are we that close to a town?' Fresh drinking water must mean some kind of purification system.

'We've never been more than a day's walk from some kind of settlement,' Forrester answered, so casually that at first Bernadette didn't react.

Then a slow anger began to build in her. 'I see,' she said quietly, setting her unfinished meal aside. 'Strange that you never saw fit to inform me of that fact.'

Forrester shrugged and kept shovelling food into his mouth. 'I didn't consider it essential that you know,' he remarked after a moment. 'Besides, nun or no nun, you're a female, and you'd have pestered me morning, noon, and night if you'd known how close we were to restaurants, air conditioning, and indoor plumbing.'

Bernadette told herself that such an arrogant,

chauvinistic comment wasn't deserving of a response and tried to keep a lid on her temper. Her clothes looked dry enough to put on, so she used that as an excuse to move away from him. He'd been right again, damn him to hell and gone; the jeans and cotton shirt *did* smell like smoke. Did the insufferable know-it-all *never* make a mistake? she fumed as she ducked behind a tree to change.

Her socks and the elastic of her bra were still slightly damp, but considering the way she perspired in this climate it would have been a waste of time to wait until they were completely dry. She knelt to retie the laces of her chunky but comfortable S.A.S. Oxfords, strapping on the gunbelt without even thinking about it, and walked back to where Forrester was pouring river water on the smouldering remains of the fire. He looked up when she thrust his neatly folded shirt under his nose.

'Thanks for the loan. Hadn't we better be going? We can't have covered more than five of our thirty miles today.'

He frowned at her short, clipped speech. 'What on earth's eating you, now?'

Bernadette drew a deep breath, then released it in a rush. 'Nothing. Not a thing,' she snapped. 'Just chalk it up to my perverse feminine nature.'

She turned on her heel with a precision that made his mouth twitch, then marched off into the bushes. On the way back, she nearly tripped over a small mound of mewling fur, halting in stunned amazement. Hanging back a little, apprehension making her cautious, she edged closer, finally kneeling beside the creature. Huge topaz eyes gazed at her fearfully, and another plaintive cry rose from its throat. It was a lion cub! she realised in astonishment, and it couldn't be more than a few weeks old.

'Well, hello there. What are you doing out here all by yourself, fella?' she murmured as she reached out to gently stroke its head.

The cub's hiss was instinctive as it flinched, but Bernadette was no stranger to claw marks and bites, and she didn't shy away. At one time or another, either

her brothers or herself had kept just about every kind of
pet it was legal to own, and she'd been bitten and
scratched by far more intimidating animals than this
adorable, pathetically frightened baby. Frowning, she
hesitated a moment, and then scooped the cub up
carefully, keeping its paws turned away from her, and
hurried back towards camp. After a single squawling
protest, he seemed to accept his fate with good grace
and fell silent.

'Look what I found,' she announced as she came in
sight of Forrester. 'The poor little thing was out there
all alone, and I thought he might belong to that lioness
the Bantu killed. Isn't he just the cutest——'

'Put him down!'

The command was issued in a voice that expected
immediate and unquestioning obedience. Bernadette's
mouth set obstinately.

'Why? Neither of us is afraid of the other, and I *do*
know how to hold him . . . see?'

Forrester's pale eyes blazed and he suddenly moved.
Not towards her, as Bernadette half expected, but to the
right, towards where his rifle lay propped against his
pack.

'I won't tell you again, Bernie, put him down,' he
ordered as he hefted it and released the safety.

If he'd yelled at her, or sworn, or even just clenched
his teeth and fixed her with a furious glare, Bernadette
might have argued. But his voice was low and perfectly
controlled, and the fact that he'd forgotten to call her
'Sister' made her instantly aware of the charged tension
in him. She bent and carefully sat the cub on its feet,
then looked into his grim face.

'What's wrong?'

'Now move away from him. *Slowly!*' he growled
when she took a hasty step in compliance.

Bernadette halted altogether for a second, then began
edging away, following the direction of his brusque
gesture.

'Colonel! what is it? He's only a baby, for heaven's
sake! And probably an orphan, on top of it.'

'I doubt it,' Forrester muttered. The rifle was held in

a light, seemingly careless two-hand grip across his body as his eyes swept the brush from which she'd emerged. 'The lioness killed yesterday was well past her prime, too old to hunt any more. That's why she'd resorted to killing Bantu livestock.'

Bernadette went cold with fear, but kept slowly putting more distance between herself and the cub, which had started crying pitifully again—for its mother, who was no doubt at that moment searching for her missing child.

'What—What are we going to do?' she asked shakily, her mouth and throat dry.

'Leave him here for his mama to find. She probably left him to fetch them both some lunch, and he wandered off. Be a good girl and get into your pack, and we'll be on our way.'

His voice was still low, calm and level, reassuring her that everything would be all right if she'd just do as he said, and some of Bernadette's fear receded. She trusted him implicitly, knew without having to think about it that he would somehow extricate them from the situation she'd created by her thoughtlessness.

'Shall I carry your pack?' she offered. She didn't see how he could get it and hold the rifle at the same time.

Before Forrester could answer, a blood-curdling, bowel-loosening roar erupted from the brush beside where Bernadette had placed the cub. Mama Lion had arrived, and she wasn't a bit pleased to find her baby in the care of two humans. Bernadette froze with her pack half on, her arms pinned inside the straps, her knees suddenly trembling and her heart in her mouth.

'Don't move!' Forrester growled the totally unnecessary order out of the side of his mouth. 'Finish pulling on your pack, and then pretend you're a tree.' When Bernadette had obediently shrugged her arms the rest of the way through the straps, he murmured, 'Good girl. All right, now take a slow, careful step towards me. If she doesn't move, take another, and then another.'

His softly spoken instructions made Bernadette wonder how he could possibly be watching both her and the brush at the same time. He seemed to be staring

straight ahead, yet he'd known to tell her to finish
pulling on her pack, and also known the precise instant
when she had.

'What if she *does* move?' she whispered as her left
foot inched across the ground.

'Let me worry about that, hmm? That's good,
now——'

He didn't finish the sentence, because Mama Lion
chose that moment to end the speculation about
whether or not she would move. The undergrowth
rustled and stirred as she stalked through it, low to the
ground, and then her head and shoulders appeared,
powerful muscles bulging as she crouched to spring.
Bernadette didn't scream as the lioness came off the
ground at her, nor did she panic and take to her heels.
Disbelief and a sense of awed wonder at the animal's
breathtaking beauty held her rooted to the spot.

Forrester's rifle roared once, and the shell caught the
attacking lioness in the centre of her chest. All four feet
had already left the ground, and the impetus of her leap
carried her forward nearly ten feet before she landed a
scant yard in front of Bernadette.

She stared down at the tawny body, and slow tears
began to trickle down her cheeks. Then she started to
shake uncontrollably as the stark reality of what had
just happened belatedly hit her. She wasn't aware of
Forrester speaking to her, and when his arms slipped
around her she stood stiff and numb inside them as the
shaking continued. His hands stroked her back, gentle,
soothing and calming, his low, gravelly voice assuring
her that it was all right, that it was over and she didn't
have to be afraid.

'I'm sorry,' was all she could think of to say, the
words blurred and indistinct. 'I'm so sorry. I didn't
think——'

Forrester held her away a little to look into her face.
His was unusually grim, his mouth taut and white at the
corners and his nostrils pinched.

'You're sorry?' he repeated harshly. 'You just came
within a hair's breadth of being mauled—possibly
killed—and you say you're *sorry*!'

Bernadette nodded miserably as she gazed past his shoulder at the corpse of the lioness.

'She was so beautiful,' she whispered. 'She was only trying to protect her cub. If I hadn't brought him here . . .' She trailed off and drew a shuddering breath that ended in a hiccup. 'It was s-stupid of me, and I'm sorry.'

Forrester seemed to stop breathing for a moment. He stared at her as if she'd just rattled off something in Chinese, then shook his head in disbelief.

'By God,' he murmured, his voice hushed. 'You are the most incredible woman.' He lifted his hands to her face, his thumbs gently stroking the tears from her cheeks, his expression softened, his eyes warm. Bernadette felt her heart kick in reaction to that uncharacteristic warmth, but before she could give herself away his hands suddenly dropped to his sides.

'Are you all right?' he asked huskily. 'We need to get clear of this area, and quick.'

She sniffed and nodded, relieved and at the same time disappointed by his sudden withdrawal. 'I'm okay. What's the hurry, though? He's the only one left,' as she looked at the trembling, terrified cub, 'and he's certainly no threat.'

'No, but his daddy might be,' Forrester muttered as he collected his pack and tugged it on. 'Two females and a cub—there's bound to be a male lurking about somewhere, and I'd just as soon not hang around to make his acquaintance.'

When he looked around to make sure she was following, he stopped in his tracks, irritated surprise drawing his heavy brows together.

'Just what do you think you're doing?'

Bernadette looked at him over the head of the cub cradled in her arms. 'He'll die if we leave him here.'

For a moment Forrester didn't reply, his lips compressing in exasperation. Then he made a curt, impatient gesture with one hand.

'Look around you, Sister. This is Africa. Animals— and people—die all the time. It's called the law of the jungle, survival of the fittest.'

Bernadette stood her ground, calm but resolute. 'But their deaths aren't on my conscience, Colonel,' she pointed out quietly.

'That's ridiculous!'

'No, it's not. I'm already responsible for his mother's death. I can't—I *won't* leave this helpless, defenceless baby to the mercy of the scavengers who come to feed on her body.'

As if he understood every word that had been said, the cub let loose with a pitiful wail of grief, and Forrester glared at it balefully.

'He won't like being carried,' he warned curtly. 'He'll probably cover you with claw marks.'

'I don't think so,' Bernadette said, smiling down at the cub. 'But if he does, I won't mind.'

'Dear God! He's no house cat, dammit! He probably weighs close to twenty pounds, already. After a couple of miles your arms are going to feel like they're being pulled from their sockets!'

Bernadette lifted her head to look him straight in the eye. 'I won't slow you down, Colonel,' she said clearly.

Forrester snorted in disgust. 'You bloody well will, but short of shooting the little beggar, I don't suppose there's any way I'm going to convince you to leave him.'

'And you wouldn't do that,' Bernadette murmured with quiet conviction.

He scowled at her, then turned on his heel and stalked away. 'Just don't expect me to tote him for you when he gets too heavy,' he growled over his shoulder.

'I won't.'

'I've got a full pack and a rifle to carry, and damned if I'll have the little beggar messing all over the front of my shirt!'

Bernadette grinned behind his back and said nothing. He'd put on the shirt she'd used for a dressing gown while her clothes dried, and she couldn't help wondering why. It wouldn't be because the cloth still carried the scent of her body, would it?

By the time they stopped for the night the cub was ravenous, and so was Bernadette. She fed him first—a can of chopped beef—while Forrester reconnoitered the area. He returned to stand over her, feet braced apart and hands on his hips.

'So now he's sharing our food, is he?' he growled.

'I'll take it out of my half,' Bernadette murmured. She was too tired for an argument; all she wanted was to get some supper into her own stomach and then crawl into her sleeping bag.

'Like hell you will! You don't eat enough to keep a bird alive, as it is!'

Her head jerked up, her eyes flashing sparks at him. 'Don't snarl at me!' she snapped. 'Just because you've got a rock where your heart ought to be doesn't mean everybody else suffers the same lack!'

Forrester's upper lip curled in a sneer. 'Thank you so much, Sister. It's always nice to know our meagre efforts have been appreciated. Could you bear to part with Junior, there, long enough to collect some firewood, do you think?'

The top of Bernadette's head felt ready to blow off. She left the cub licking the beef can and stormed off to look for wood, furiously silent, thinking he was positively *the* most disagreeable person she'd ever met and she couldn't *wait* to be rid of him. Just when she'd begun to think there was a sensitive, caring man hidden beneath all that arrogance and cynicism, he had to go and turn mean again. Damn him, it was almost as if he was *trying* to antagonise her, *wanted* her to despise him! Surly, bad-tempered jerk! she fumed as she snatched up twigs and small branches, using the physical activity as a release for some of her anger.

When she returned, she nearly dropped the stack of wood in her arms. For a second she thought she must be seeing things. Forrester was sitting on the ground, the cub between his spread legs. He'd fashioned a nipple of sorts from a square he'd cut off one of their waterproof ground sheets and was holding it in one hand while the cub suckled greedily. When he glanced up, one dark brow quirked at Bernadette's astonished expression.

'I found some powdered milk in the supplies,' he told her casually.

She didn't know what to say. Well, she did, actually. An apology seemed to be called for, but she knew the words would stick in her throat.

'That was very thoughtful of you, Colonel,' she managed grudgingly as she laid the wood down and avoided looking directly at him.

But she couldn't avoid him forever, and when she eventually forced herself to turn in his direction there was a suspicious gleam in Forrester's eyes.

'A compliment, Sister?' he drawled in feigned surprise.

Bernadette's back went stiff and she didn't respond as she opened her pack and started taking out food.

'What do you think, Leo?' he asked the cub soberly. 'She doesn't *look* feverish, does she?'

Bernadette tried to stay angry with him, but found it was impossible. The idea of Colonel Sam Forrester, veteran of Lord knew how many minor wars and skirmishes, sitting in the middle of the jungle playing nanny to an orphaned lion cub——! She kept her face averted to hide an involuntary smile.

'Cat got your tongue?' he drawled.

Her movements stilled and she bent her head to study her clasped hands, still smiling.

'No. I'm just practising meekness,' she murmured, and heard his soft chuckle.

'How do you like it?'

'Not much,' she admitted drily, then closed her eyes and tried to work up an appetite for crow. 'I apologise for being insulting and short-tempered before. It was uncharitable and unChristian of me,' she recited stiffly.

Forrester's mocking voice at her back made her jump. 'And God knows what that cost you. But I thank you for making the effort, Sister . . . from the bottom of my rock.'

A spontaneous laugh erupted from Bernadette, and was swiftly followed by his husky chortle. She looked over her shoulder at him, kneeling behind her, and he unexpectedly reached out to muss her short hair as if she was some precocious child.

'I don't know about you, but I'm starved,' he said

with a grin. 'Let's eat, before young Leo cleans out the rest of our supplies.'

They prepared the meal together, and when it was finished they sat by the fire in companionable silence and watched the cub's tentative explorations.

'We'll be coming to a small mining town early tomorrow morning,' Forrester murmured after a while as he took out his pistol and began the ritual of cleaning it.

Bernadette digested that in silence, then asked: 'If it's that close, why didn't we go on in tonight?'

He gave her a narrow sidelong glance, his hands never faltering in their task. 'Ever been to a mining town, Sister?' he drawled. Bernadette shook her head no, and one corner of his mouth lifted wryly. 'I thought not. They're full of bored, hard-working, harder-drinking men who are usually starved for the sight of a woman. Any woman,' he stressed softly. 'Even one who looks like a half-grown boy and claims to be a nun.'

'Sounds like the perfect vacation spot,' Bernadette muttered, and he grinned. 'Am I to be cast in the role of your woman again—the one you shot the rich Frenchman to procure?'

Forrester laughed softly. 'It worked once, and my motto is: If it works, don't mess with it.'

'And you honestly expect these miners to believe you went to such trouble for a woman who looks like a half-grown boy?' she asked drily.

He shot her another amused glance. 'Careful, Sister, your feminine ego is showing.'

Bernadette wisely decided to change the subject. 'What about Leo?'

Forrester finished wiping the pistol and slid it back into its holster, then laid the gunbelt on top of his pack.

'Worried about what's to become of the little beggar, are you? I could point out that you should have thought of that sooner,' he drawled, then glanced at her mutinous expression and half smiled. 'But I won't. As it happens, I know a man in the town we're headed for who occasionally picks up extra money by providing wild animals for a park in Florida. I'm sure George will jump at the chance to sell them such a fine specimen as our Leo, and he'll receive excellent care and a safe home for the rest of his life.'

Bernadette's eyes glowed with happiness and she positively beamed at him. 'Oh, Sam what a perfect solution! Did you hear that, Leo?' She turned to the cub, unaware that she'd used his given name for the first time, or of the change that came over him when he heard it on her lips. 'You're going to live in Florida! Orange trees, ocean air ... *Disney World*!'

She laughed with delight, and didn't notice that Forrester had risen and walked a little distance away, his hands thrust deep in his pockets as he stood with his back to her. He looked like a man who had just said goodbye to something—or someone—very precious to him.

CHAPTER SEVEN

WHEN they entered the town at about eight o'clock the next morning, Bernadette experienced a feeling of unreality, as if she was dreaming the whole thing. The place couldn't actually exist, except maybe on the back lot of some Hollywood movie studio.

The main street was lined with run-down clapboard buildings, the paint peeling and windows boarded up where the glass was missing. The asphalt of the street itself had cracked and sunken to form potholes a horse could get lost in, a result of the seasonal torrential rains in this part of the world. Altogether, the place could hardly be called a garden spot, she thought glumly as she stuck close to Forrester's side, the cub clasped protectively to her breast.

'George's place is at the other end of town,' he told her as he stepped over a pile of debris in front of one of the open doorways. 'We'll stock up on supplies first, then drop Leo off with him.'

And then just keep right on going, Bernadette hoped with all her heart. She followed him silently, since he seemed to know where he was heading, but her eyes constantly darted from side to side, alert for some kind of threat or menace.

He stopped at a building that appeared to house a sort of general store, standing aside to let Bernadette pass in front of him. She'd barely set foot inside before a raucous voice ordered her back out.

' 'ere, now, 'alt right whur ye be, lad! Oi ain't 'avin' 'at wild beastie in 'ere among me foodstuffs! Out! Out wi' ye, oi say!'

Bernadette stood in the middle of the floor and blinked. The language the old crone behind the counter spoke sounded vaguely like English, but the only word she could be sure she'd understood had been 'out!' She glanced over her shoulder at Forrester in uncertainty.

'It's all right, Aggie, they're with me,' he drawled as he came forward.

Besides having a serious speech impediment, the old woman was apparently blind and deaf, as well. Her eyes squinted to slits and she twisted her balding white head to one side, her wrinkled face screwed up with the effort of both seeing and hearing at the same time.

' 'ere, oozat?' she screeched, then cackled with glee. 'Sam Forrester, oi might've knowed! Oo else'd 'ave the brass t'bring a lion cub an' a 'half-growed boy inta this 'ell-'ole!'

Forrester's appreciative laugh caused Bernadette's cheeks to burn as he spared her a wicked grin and stepped closer to the old woman.

'Watch your language, Aggie,' he bellowed into her face, then jerked a thumb toward Bernadette. 'That one's a lady.'

The woman guffawed in obvious disbelief as she cast a knowing leer upon him. 'Lady, my arse! Wot the 'ell would a lady be doin' wi' a black'earted villain loik you?'

Bernadette took a belated but intense liking to the dried up old hag, and her smile was sweet as Forrester cocked one eyebrow at her in amusement.

'I think I'll wait outside with Leo, while you conclude your business,' she told him *sotto voce*.

'Good idea,' he drawled. 'It might take a while to make her understand what I want. But don't go far.'

She had no intention of venturing beyond what passed for a pavement at the front of the store, but she saw no need to tell him so. By the time he appeared in the door and motioned her back inside, Bernadette was more than ready to go. She'd been the recipient of several interested looks, which shouldn't have been surprising, considering she was probably the only woman under fifty for miles around and was standing on the town's main street holding a lion in her arms. Still, she was relieved to be able to rejoin him and the old woman inside.

He took the cub from her while she shrugged out of her pack, then loaded it with the remainder of the supplies he'd purchased. All the while, the grinning Aggie kept them both under her squint-eyed, knowing stare.

'Don't stay away s'long next time, Sam,' she urged as she followed them to the door. 'An' bring yer lady wi' ye when ye come again.'

'What a character,' Bernadette remarked as she tried to keep pace with his long-legged stride.

'Aggie? She's an original, all right. Her husband worked in the copper mines. When he died, she stayed and went to work managing the company store. The miners like and respect her, and since she took charge there's been less loss through theft. It's worked out well for everyone.'

Bernadette was silent as she walked along at his side. Just a few days ago she'd have been surprised to discover that he took an interest in the lives of a bunch of copper miners in a company town that probably wasn't even on any map. Now that fact didn't surprise her at all, but the obvious affection in his deep voice when he spoke of the old woman Aggie did. It also gave her a warm, pleased feeling. He was turning out to be much more than she'd thought at first, with depths to him she hadn't begun to suspect.

His friend George was yet another surprise. A short, squat man with biceps almost as big as Bernadette's waist and a patch over his left eye, he had the boisterous temperament to go with his thatch of orange hair and ruddy complexion. He greeted Forrester by lifting him off the floor in a bear hug that would probably have snapped the spine of a lesser man, and then dropped him and roared with laughter as he aimed a ham-sized fist at the Colonel's chin.

Bernadette gasped audibly. It had come so unexpectedly, so suddenly, that she knew Forrester was destined to suffer a broken jaw and several loose teeth, at the very least. The cub yowled in protest as her arms tightened around him reflexively.

But the thunk of fist meeting jaw she waited for never came. Forrester ducked at the last possible moment, and the next thing she knew he had the other man in a stranglehold from behind, his lean forearm pressing into George's throat. Bernadette stared, totally dumbfounded. They were both laughing their fool heads off.

'You're slipping, George,' Forrester accused as he released the man and stepped back. 'Five years ago you'd have been ready for that.'

'Unfortunately age takes its toll on us all,' George agreed amiably, then grinned and punched the Colonel's shoulder. 'Except you, you obnoxious son of a hyena! You're looking meaner than ever, rot your soul! What brings you all the way out here? No, wait, let me guess—is it the fuss the government's making over Jimbo's secession?'

'Indirectly,' Forrester drawled. Turning towards Bernadette, he held out a hand. 'But I also brought you a little something I thought you might find a use for.'

As she put her hand in his and stepped forward, the other man noticed her for the first time. His one good eye went wide with appreciation and he gave a low, lascivious chuckle.

'Oh, yes, my friend, offhand I can think of several uses for such a welcome gift.'

'The cub, George,' Forrester muttered, taking it from Bernadette to shove it into his beefy arms. Then he pulled her against his side and cupped his hand to the curve of her hip. 'This one's not on offer. Bernie, meet George Feeney, the meanest, raunchiest, most foul-mouthed drunken bum to ever come out of Kilkenny.'

Bernadette smiled nervously, thinking it was a wonder the man didn't take another swing at him. But George only chuckled and reached out to clasp her hand in a hairy paw.

'Pleased ter meet you, Bernie,' he said with a grin, then waved his arm at the door behind him. 'Go on in and make yourselve's t'home. I'll just take this little beggar out back and have Molly get him settled in.'

'Do we have to——' Bernadette began in a whisper as George disappeared down a narrow hallway.

'He's a friend,' Forrester interrupted quietly. 'He's offered us his hospitality, and I won't offend him by refusing. Relax, nothing's going to happen to you here.'

And that was that, she thought resentfully as he urged her towards the door with a hand at her back: the great Sam Forrester had spoken; his will be done.

The crowd in the large, square room they entered consisted of roughly four men to every woman, she estimated. Some smoked, most had a drink in their hand, and a few couples were shuffling listlessly to the music that issued from a large radio perched precariously on a corner of one of the hand-hewn tables. It took a second or two for her to realise that half the dancing couples were made up of two men, and she couldn't keep herself from staring as Forrester led her to an unoccupied table and helped her off with her pack.

'No, they aren't,' he drawled as he shucked his as well and pulled a chair close to hers. 'It's just that there's a dire shortage of women hereabouts, so if you want to dance, you pretty much have to settle for whatever partner's available.'

'Oh,' Bernadette murmured in chagrin. 'But . . . what are they all doing here, now? It can't be past nine in the morning.'

Forrester didn't answer until he'd smiled a thank-you at the voluptuous girl who placed two mugs of beer in front of them and taken a long swig from his.

'They work the graveyard shift. Midnight to eight in the morning,' he explained when Bernadette just stared at him in confusion. 'They come here for an hour or so after work to unwind and heft a few pints, then go to their rooms and sleep until it's time to go back to the mines. It's a hell of a way to make a living,' he observed drily, then lifted his mug again to drain half its contents in one thirsty swallow.

'Why do they do it—choose to live like this?' she asked with a frown. 'It must be a terribly depressing existence.'

'Money,' he answered succinctly. 'The pay's top notch, and most of them only stay a few years, until they've saved up a nice little nest egg. Then they go back home—wherever that may be—marry the girl next door, and settle down to raise five or six squawling brats. It is my considered opinion that they lose something in the bargain.'

Bernadette smiled tightly at his cynical sarcasm. 'You don't believe in marriage?' she challenged softly.

He shrugged and finished off his beer, then reached for hers. 'I've yet to see a man who benefited from it,' he drawled. 'Oh, I'll grant you it's great for the woman. She gets a free ride all the way, while poor old hubby has to work his butt off to keep her in the style she figures she deserves. And I've noticed that something seems to happen to a woman once she gets her hook set in a man,' he went on thoughtfully. 'Even the sweetest, most eager-to-please young thing turns mean the minute she's got that ring on her finger.' He grimaced. 'The poor beggar's got to give up all his pastimes, his friends, devote himself exclusively to keeping the little woman happy, until he's so damned miserable all he wants is out.'

When his little speech was finished, Bernadette propped an elbow on the table and rested her chin in her hand, staring at him while he stared into his beer. Or rather, her beer.

'For an intelligent man, you can say some of the most preposterous, asinine things I've ever heard in my life,' she told him levelly.

Forrester glanced up and met her eyes, and a slow smile spread over his face. 'Yeah, I know.'

In that instant he looked more like a wayward, mischief-making boy than the tough cynic she knew him to be. His eyes glittered with devilment, and his smile bordered on being a rakehell grin. Bernadette responded with a purely impulsive smile of her own, shaking her head at him.

'Some woman must have really done a number on you, somewhere along the line,' she remarked pensively.

Forrester gave her a narrow-eyed look and opened his mouth to answer, but just then George appeared at their table and swung an empty chair around to join them.

'That is one fine cub, Samuel,' he said to Forrester. 'What do I owe you for him?'

'Not a darn thing,' Forrester answered with a decisive shake of his head. 'Bernie bagged him, and all she wants is for him to have a good home. She's incredibly tender-hearted where homeless orphans are concerned,' he added wryly.

George ignored the last. 'I can promise, he will have,' he assured Bernadette, and she gave him a grateful smile. He sat back in his chair and regarded her in silence for a while. She suspected he was wondering what she was doing with Forrester, but she knew he wouldn't ask. He was the sort of man who respected other people's privacy, and expected the same consideration in return. Finally he leaned forward again, resting his huge arms on the table.

'So. You'll both stay for lunch, of course.'

Forrester reluctantly shook his head. 'Sorry, George, no can do,' he said quietly as he met the other man's eyes.

George nodded in understanding. 'So it's like that, is it?' He released a heavy sigh. 'Sam, Sam, will you ever tire of this love affair with death and dying?' Turning to Bernadette, he tilted his head towards Forrester with a grimace. 'For years I've tried to convince him he's too old to keep fighting other people's wars, that he should find himself a good woman and make a home somewhere. But will he listen?' He made a sound of disgust in his throat. 'Oh, no, not that one. He won't be satisfied 'til he gets himself blown to smithereens fighting somebody else's lost cause.'

Forrester suddenly pushed the mug he was holding away and got to his feet.

'This conversation's too morbid for my taste,' he drawled. 'Come on, let's dance.'

Bernadette wasn't given the option of refusal as he pulled her out of her chair and on to the middle of the floor.

'Don't worry, I don't expect Ginger Rogers,' he growled in her ears as he swept her close. 'Just put your arms around my neck and plaster yourself up against me.'

'I'll do no such thing! Have you completely lost your

mind!' Bernadette hissed, blushing to the roots of her hair as every eye in the room seemed to turn in their direction.

'You're supposed to be my woman, remember?' he taunted as he easily thwarted her efforts to put a little space between them. 'For your own protection, Sister——'

'Don't give me that!' She forced a smile for the benefit of their audience, but the words were whispered furiously through clenched teeth. 'You said nothing would happen here, and you were right. Now let me *go*!'

Forrester grinned down at her as he lifted her hands to his shoulders. 'Okay,' he drawled, unaffected by her trembling rage. 'Maybe you're right, and they wouldn't lay a finger on you. Maybe. Look on it as pandering to my fragile male ego, then. I do have a certain reputation to maintain, you know. Try to look as though you've found heaven in my arms, as if I'm everything you've ever dreamed of in a man. Use your imagination, Sister.'

Bernadette had gone white, her eyes two huge violet pools brimming with frustrated tears.

'You're thoroughly detestable,' she whispered shakily. 'You take such unholy pleasure in humiliating me, don't you . . . mocking me and tormenting me, knowing I can't fight back on your level?'

Her voice wavered huskily, and as he gazed down into her brimming eyes, Forrester's jaw tensed and he drew a sharp breath. At least half of her reaction was caused by the pain of stifling sexual awareness and response, but he couldn't know that. The hands he'd placed on his broad shoulders itched to climb around his neck, and her muscles were taut with the effort of holding herself away from him, when all she wanted was to lean into his hard body and feel it respond to her nearness. But the consequences if she should give into her own almost overwhelming urges didn't bear thinking about.

He exhaled harshly and brought a rough hand up to force her head down to his chest. All the mockery had

gone out of him; he was tense and stonily silent as he
guided her slowly around the floor. Bernadette soon
realised what had wrought such a swift change in him.
It had been that single word 'unholy' that did it. It had
reminded him of who—*what*—she was supposed to be,
and now *he* was angry. At her, or himself?

'You may not fight back on my level,' he finally
muttered, 'but by God you manage to connect with
some damned crippling blows now and then. You know
what the problem is, don't you?' he asked when she
didn't respond. 'The reason I'm such a bastard to you
sometimes?'

Bernadette knew. Oh, yes, she most certainly knew.
At that very moment, believing she was a nun and with
a couple of dozen witnesses present, if she'd given him
the slightest encouragement he'd have started making
love to her, right there in that smoky, crowded room.
And, heaven help her, she'd have let him; if she was
honest, more than just let him.

'Bernie?' he said in that harsh-soft voice that
whispered across her senses like velvet.

Thinking that if she answered maybe she could
forestall him saying it aloud, she nodded, not lifting her
head. 'Yes,' she said in a husky, breathless voice. 'I
know.'

He relaxed a little, but paradoxically his arms pressed
her even closer, making her aware of him in a way she
didn't want to be aware, a way that was shattering,
dangerously undermining her self-control.

'I thought so,' he murmured, mocking amusement
deepening his voice and intensifying its effect on her.
His head dipped, and his mouth was suddenly right
next to her ear.

'How I want you,' he breathed, and Bernadette's
throat closed, trapping her breath, while every last
ounce of strength drained out of her and left her with
knees turned suddenly to rubber.

'I've never said that to a nun before,' he mused wryly.
'But then I've never met a nun like you. I doubt anyone
has. What business has a woman like you got *being* a
nun!'

Bernadette couldn't have responded to that if her life had depended on it, but fortunately he went on without waiting for her to.

'I know,' he mocked. 'I just answered my own question. Well, don't let it bother you, Sister. It's my problem, and I'll deal with it.' He leaned back a little to give her a cynical smile. 'And try not to be too shocked. If you knew about some of my really major sins, you'd realise what a trivial transgression lust actually is.'

Trivial? Maybe to him, but Bernadette felt as if her calm, well-ordered existence had been shattered beyond repair. If only she really *was* a nun, she thought with a touch of hysteria, this impossibly complicated situation would never have developed. As it was, she felt trapped in a maze from which there was no obvious exit.

He wanted her. A simple enough fact, on the surface. And she knew she wanted him in exactly the same way—had, ever since that sizzling, heart-stopping moment two nights ago when he'd virtually lain on top of her inside a sleeping bag and she'd experienced a desire so unexpected and devastatingly intense that just the memory of it made her tremble in fear.

Virginal terror. Was that what it was? She rejected the notion as soon as it occurred. In this day and age, when you got slapped in the face with sex every time you opened a magazine or turned on your television set? No, it wasn't the thought of making love that frightened her—it was *him*!

He was like no man she'd ever known before: tough, yes; a cynic, definitely; harbouring a latent cruel streak, possibly; and positively-without-a-doubt his own man, in every way. She'd been warned about him, more than once, by people who should know, He would never be tamed, brought to heel, made into a domestic animal; not by her or anyone else. He'd already stated his views on marriage, so what did that leave? A brief, tempestuous affair, no doubt glorious and passionately intense, but over the minute he grew bored or his thirst for adventure needed to be slaked?

Bernadette knew herself too well to believe she'd be satisfied with anything less than a long-term commit-

ment. And she also knew—instinctively—that she'd
never get anything like 'forever' from Sam Forrester.

When he suddenly muttered in her ear she jerked
against him in surprise.

'Don't look around, but we just got some unwelcome
company.'

Bernadette had to force herself not to swivel her
head, and her fingers unconsciously curled to grip his
shoulders.

'Government soldiers?' she whispered anxiously.

'More likely mercenaries on the government payroll.'
He swore under his breath, and Bernadette's head came
up, her eyes fixed anxiously on his taut features.
'They're mercenaries, all right. I recognise a couple of
them.'

If he recognised them, it only stood to reason that they
might recognise him, as well. It took a determined
effort to keep her voice from rising in panic.

'What are we going to do?'

'Go back to the table, have a couple of beers, and
then get the hell out of here.' He glanced down at her,
frowning slightly. 'Don't go to pieces on me, for God's
sake. Just follow my lead, and we'll be out of here
before you know it. All right?'

Bernadette nodded mutely, and got a brief squeeze in
reward as he curved an arm around her waist to lead
her back to their table.

George was gone, and so were their packs and the
rifle, but the same curvaceous girl who'd delivered their
beers appeared with a tray bearing two fresh mugs as
they reached the table. Say what you would about the
clientele, Bernadette thought, the service here couldn't
be faulted.

There was a slip of paper on the tray. Forrester
palmed it under cover of some flirtatious banter with
the girl, and read what was on it as he let his hand fall
to his lap. Then he casually made a fist, and the
crumpled paper was slipped to their waitress along with
a suggestive smile and a lewd wink. Bernadette glared at
him, even though she knew the subterfuge was
necessary, under the circumstances. His reaction was

typical: he laughed in her face and openly fondled the other girl's ample *derrière* as it swayed past him.

'Not bad,' he drawled as he pushed one of the mugs in front of Bernadette. 'But let's not overdo it, shall we? A little jealousy's a nice touch, but you look as if you'd like to spit in my eye.'

She gave him a saccharine smile and lifted the frosty mug in both hands. 'Can we please get out of here?' she murmured over the rim. 'Those men are making me nervous.'

There were five of them, sitting together near the door, muttering to each other and casting low-browed glances in their direction. They wore field dress, and had identical black berets tilted towards their foreheads.

There presence didn't seem to concern Forrester as he drank deeply from his beer and cocked a dark brow at her to indicate that she should do likewise. Bernadette took another sip, surreptitiously stealing a glance at the quintet across the room. To her horror, one of them rose and began walking straight towards their table. She gasped and nearly choked on her beer. The Colonel reached over and calmly took the mug from her trembling hand before it tipped and dumped its contents in her lap.

'Easy does it,' he murmured, then set his own mug aside, freeing his hands as the other man stopped beside the table.

'Colonel Forrester.' The man's eyes met his briefly as he uttered the stiffly polite greeting, then shifted to Bernadette. 'My friends and I recognised you at once, of course. We were wondering what business you and the charming lady could possibly have here?'

'We're on our honeymoon,' Forrester drawled without batting an eye, and Bernadette nearly swallowed her tongue.

The soldier's mouth twisted in an uncertain smile. 'In that case, you must join us for a drink. We would all like to toast the lovely . . . bride.'

Bernadette's heart stopped, then slid sickeningly downward. Her frantic eyes sought Forrester's, but he was looking at the mercenary with mild disgust, apparently still unconcerned as he lounged in the hard chair, both hands in plain sight on top of the table.

'Thanks, but no,' he said in a level, barely audible growl.

The other man's mouth tightened, his gazed fastened on Bernadette's pale face. 'I must insist,' he said coldly.

Menace hung in the air, heavy and oppressive. Bernadette could almost smell it as the seconds ticked by and Forrester said nothing more. Finally she heard him heave a slightly impatient sigh.

'Some people just can't leave well enough alone,' he muttered under his breath. Bernadette swung her head towards him, and noticed that George had returned and was talking to a group of the miners at the other side of the room. She impulsively started to tell him.

'Sam——'

'Yes, darling, I know,' he interrupted smoothly. 'Excuse me, will you, this won't take a moment.'

Her mouth was still hanging open when the table suddenly tipped, then crashed on to its side, and Forrester went over it as if it wasn't there. Bernadette jumped out of her chair and then just stood there, too stunned to move as the sound of splintering wood rose above the Abba song playing on the radio.

Then she saw the other four mercenaries leap out of their seats, and fear for Forrester unlocked her frozen limbs. She rushed into the fray at the same time as several of the miners, and was almost immediately knocked on her backside for her trouble.

By the time she crawled clear of the forest of legs and scrambled to her feet, a full-scale brawl was underway. Unable to even see Sam for the other combatants surrounding him, she shoved her way to one of the vacated tables and climbed on top of it. She spotted him at once, a lean arm locked around the neck of one of the mercenaries and a handful of hair in one of his fists.

'Way to go, Sam!' she yelled in encouragement. 'Give it to him, good! Mop up the floor with him!'

His head snapped around, and when he saw her his jaw sagged in astonishment. Then he snapped it shut and glared at her furiously.

'You little idiot! Get down from there now, before you—Oof!'

Bernadette gasped as the other man took advantage of his distraction to ram a balled fist into his middle. Before Forrester could recover, his opponent followed through with an uppercut to his chin, sending him staggering backward on his heels.

He lurched to a halt a foot in front of Bernadette, wheezing and holding a hand to his stomach, and the man came after him with a triumphant laugh. Bernadette glanced around frantically for some kind of weapon. The only thing handy was an empty beer mug. She snatched it up just as the mercenary closed in on Sam and delivered a solid right cross to his jaw, sending him into a spin. He collapsed heavily on to the table, his arms spread, shaking his head to clear it. Bernadette dropped to her knees in front of him while the grinning mercenary took a moment to savour the anticipation of his victory.

'*Sam*! Sam, for God's sake, get up!' she urged impatiently. 'You're not going to let that creep come out on top, are you?'

He lifted his head to frown at her groggily, a thin trickle of blood at one corner of his mouth, and the other man picked that moment to reach for his shoulder to spin him back around.

'Oh, for——' Bernadette muttered, and without thinking she swung the mug as hard as she could at his face.

It connected with a force that jarred her shoulder and temporarily numbed her fingers, but all she cared about was the fact that he seemed to have temporarily abandoned his assault. If she'd spared him a glance, she'd have understood why. His eyes glazed and he swayed on his feet, then crumpled gracefully to the floor.

'*Sam!*' She exhorted, grasping a handful of his hair and tugging impatiently. What had become of the superbly fit career soldier with the lightning reflexes? she wondered irritably. He lay sprawled across the table like a comatose wino, his legs splayed to half support him and his stern jaw slack under its five-day growth of beard.

'Will you get *up*!'

She shoved at his shoulder, and he grunted and lifted his head, then got an elbow under him and pushed himself to his feet.

'What——!' He glanced over his shoulder, his body miraculously assuming its normal upright, alert and ready stance. 'What happened!'

He turned back to Bernadette, his eyes narrowing Then he reached out and uncurled her fingers from the handle of the mug. When he held it in front of her face she saw that—apart from a small shard attached to it— the handle was all that was left. Her eyes grew round and her mouth gaped open.

'My word! Did I do that?'

'Nobody else,' he drawled, then laughed as he dropped the piece of glass and grasped her waist to lift her off the table.

'Come on. This way.'

He half dragged her to a narrow door at the back of the room, then through it into a partially enclosed space at the rear of the building, where a Jeep was waiting. Their packs and Forrester's rifle had been stashed behind the seats.

'You drive. I'll ride shotgun,' he ordered brusquely.

Bernadette hurried around the Jeep to climb behind the wheel, and the engine turned over smoothly on the first try.

'You *do* know how to drive one of these things?' Forrester asked as he slid in beside her.

Bernadette turned her head to flash him a quick, absolutely devilish grin. 'Is the Pope Catholic?'

Then she rammed the gearshift into first and popped the clutch, and he was thrown back against his seat with a muttered, 'Oh, no!'

'Get back on the main road, than just follow it out of town,' he instructed as he reached behind him for the rifle.

They were halfway to the trees which marked the town's boundaries when gunfire broke out behind them.

Bernadette risked taking her eyes off the crumbling road long enough to glance worriedly at Sam. On his knees, facing backward, he was removing a pair of wire-rimmed glasses from the case he'd taken from his shirt pocket. He slipped them on while her eyes darted back and forth between him and the road.

'You need glasses?' she asked as he propped his left elbow on the back of his seat and braced the rifle against his right shoulder.

'Only for accuracy at long range.' His voice was cool, his attention devoted to sighting down the barrel as he rested his cheek against the stock.

Bernadette went pale, her knuckles white on the steering wheel. 'Oh, my God,' she whispered.

'If you're offering up a prayer, I suggest you keep it short,' Forrester muttered. 'And stop swerving all over the bloody road.'

She swallowed hard and tried to concentrate on keeping the Jeep on as steady a course as possible while still avoiding the worst of the potholes. She was so intent on the virtually impossible task, she failed to notice that the road abruptly ended at the edge of the town. The Jeep's tyres left the asphalt and a second later they made a bone-jarring landing on the rutted dirt track beyond it.

'Careful, Bernie!' Forester growled in complaint.

'I'm *sorry*!' she said wildly. 'I'm doing the best I can! Are they still shooting at us?' She didn't dare look around to see, and the pounding of her pulse in her ears combined with the whine of the engine drowned out any sound more than a few feet away.

'Of course they're still shooting at us! Bloody fools must be half blind, though,' he added contemptuously. 'They haven't come within ten feet of us, yet.'

No sooner had the words left his mouth than a bullet whistled past Bernadette's right ear.

'*Sam!*'

'Slow down and hold her steady for two seconds,' he ordered curtly.

She eased off the accelerator and did her best to keep

the Jeep pointed straight ahead, and then nearly sideswiped a tree when the crack of his rifle caught her by surprise.

There was a sharp bend in the road up ahead. If she could just get them around it, they should be home free. As far as she knew, bullets always followed a straight trajectory. Risking Forrester's wrath, she shifted into third and stomped down hard on the accelerator, aiming for the inside edge of the curve.

He swore viciously, but she ignored him, all her concentration on the job at hand. As they hurtled into the turn she remembered all the stories she'd ever heard about Jeeps flipping over, pinning the occupants inside, killing or crippling them for life. She considered praying, but before words could form in her mind the curve was behind them.

'Nice going, Sister,' Forrester drawled. 'I may enter you at Le Mans next year.'

Bernadette didn't answer. White-faced and slightly nauseous, she was afraid she'd become hysterical if she tried to speak.

'You want to slow this thing down a little?' he suggested after a moment. 'Or were you trying for a new land speed record?'

Bernadette realised with a jolt that her foot still had the accelerator pinned to the floor, and she lifted it at once. She was breathing hard, and her heart was racing with residual fear.

'Will they come after us?' she asked anxiously.

'If they do, it'll be on foot. George will disable every vehicle in town, if he has to.' He waited a moment, then said quietly, 'Be watching for a place to pull over. We've got a slight problem, here.'

Bernadette's head jerked around and she cried out sharply. His right hand was clamped over the sleeve of his shirt, high on the left arm, and bright red blood was seeping through his fingers.

'Oh, Sam!'

'Don't panic,' he said tersely. 'It's not half as bad as it looks.' Then he suddenly threw his arms out, bracing himself against the dash. '*Bernie*! Dear God, look out! The——'

'The tree!' was probably what he meant to say, but they hit it head-on before he could get the last word out.

Bernadette was thrown on to the oversized steering wheel and the breath left her lungs in a painful rush. She was stunned for several minutes, and as clarity returned she thought ruefully that her poor ribs were taking one hell of a beating on this trip.

'Oh, Sam, I'm sorry,' she muttered as she sat back carefully, testing her body for any invisible damage. There didn't appear to be any.

'I'm usually a good driver, honest. Are you all right?'

She turned as she asked, and immediately froze in horror. He was slumped sideways in his seat, one arm dangling to the floor and his head propped against the door at a frighteningly unnatural angle. Even as she cried his name, Bernadette knew he couldn't hear her.

CHAPTER EIGHT

BERNADETTE grimly subdued her rising panic and forced herself to move, telling herself that any kind of positive action was better than just staring at him helplessly.

It was difficult to examine him for injuries inside the Jeep. If he had any fractures, at least they weren't compound; she couldn't see any bones poking through his skin or feel them through his clothes. And unfortunately that was the limit of her expertise where traumatic injury was concerned. If she'd thought of the possibility of spinal damage, or known any of the rules for dealing with it, she'd probably have huddled in her seat in impotent fear. But since she didn't, she decided to get him out of the Jeep, so he could at least stretch out.

She hurried around to Forrester's side and opened the door, stepping close to catch his head and shoulders as they fell out. When she glanced down in concern, she noticed the sprinkling of grey in the short, thick dark hair resting against her breast. Hardly surprising for a man his age. Still, the grey seemed to emphasise his vulnerability at that moment—that and the glasses, which had somehow remained in place and unbroken during the crash. Bernadette felt tears spurt to her eyes, but blinked them away in impatience. Weeping and wringing her hands wouldn't do either of them any good.

Dragging him clear of the Jeep and on to the side of the road taxed her strength to its limit, and she had to rest for a minute or two before she could do more.

That arm had to be seen to. She knew it, realised that had to come first on her list of priorities. Still, she hesitated. 'She'd seen gunshot wounds a couple of times in Belfast, knew the damage a single bullet could do to the human body, and she had no desire at all to peel away Forrester's shirt and find that his beautiful, tautly

116

muscled flesh had been mangled and torn. She had to steel herself for the job, praying that it wouldn't be too bad and that she could do the right things for him—hopefully without being sick or fainting.

By the time she'd managed to tug the bloodied shirt off, she'd worked herself into a state of near-hysteria. Her breath came in sharp, shallow gasps and her muscles ached with the tension that gripped her. Her hands trembled. She frowned at them, dismayed and angry with herself. Closing her eyes tight, she clenched her fingers into fists and forced herself to take several slow, deep breaths before she looked at his arm.

She could have wept with relief. He'd been right again: it wasn't nearly as bad as she'd feared. There was a neat, fairly shallow groove in the muscle, and it had virtually stopped bleeding all on its own. All it needed was cleaning and dressing.

When she returned to the Jeep for her pack, she saw that someone—most likely George—had wedged a bottle of Scotch whisky between it and Forrester's. She collected the bottle along with her pack, thinking of all the movies she'd seen in which whisky was used as an antiseptic/disinfectant.

The wound was easy to get to, and she had a choice of salves and ointments with which to dress it, as well as a good supply of gauze and bandages. Hesitating briefly, her bottom lip caught between her teeth, she broke the seal on the whisky and poured a liberal splash over his upper arm. It must have stung like the very devil, but Forrester's eyelids didn't even flicker. Deciding that in this case more was better, she tipped the bottle again, dousing the wound, then gently patted his arm dry and selected a tube of ointment, which she applied liberally.

By the time she'd finished she was feeling rather pleased with herself. The bandage looked neat and tidy, and there was no sign of renewed bleeding. The only thing that troubled her was the fact that Forrester hadn't regained consciousness. He should be coming around by now, shouldn't he?

She carefully removed his glasses, replaced them in

their padded case, and tucked it into his pack. Then she
knelt at his shoulder and cautiously slipped her fingers
into his springy hair, running them lightly over his
scalp, probing gently for a lump or break in his skin.
The examination could hardly be considered profes-
sional, partly because she derived so much pleasure
from the feel of his hair against her palms. At any rate,
the only thing she could find was a small knot just
behind his right ear.

Bernadette sat back and chewed her lip in indecision.
What if the mercenaries came after them? Even on foot,
it shouldn't take them long to catch up; they couldn't
be more than a mile or two from town. The hiss of
escaping steam from the Jeep's punctured radiator told
her the vehicle was now useless, and there was no way
she could carry Forrester, or for that matter move him
more than a few feet at a time. About the only thing she
could do would be to get them both off the road and
into the cover of the trees, so that at least they'd be
hidden from anyone coming down the road.

She dragged and wrestled him about fifteen feet into
the undergrowth, slipping her hands under his arms and
linking her fingers over his sparsely furred chest. Then
she went back for their packs, the rifle, and—just in
case—the bottle of Scotch. When it had all been
transferred she sank down beside him, panting from the
exertion. Her shirt stuck to her back between her
shoulders and her damp hair was plastered to her
forehead, but she wasn't even aware of the heat or her
discomfort as she gazed down at him.

He *would* come to, sooner or later, she told herself
desperately. She had no idea how much time had
elapsed since they ran into the tree. It seemed like
hours, but she knew it couldn't have been anywhere
near that long. Gradually the realisation dawned that
until Forrester *did* come around, the responsibility for
their survival was hers, and hers alone.

Her gaze slid reluctantly to the rifle, then darted
away in revulsion. Absolutely not. She doubted if she
could even manage to lift it again, much less use it, even
if she'd known how. His pistol? She gnawed at her lip

as she stared at it, still snuggled against his thigh, looking for all the world like a part of him. At least she knew it would be clean and ready to fire, but it looked almost as heavy as the rifle, and every bit as deadly.

That left her own small handgun. Forrester had cleaned and oiled it a couple of times, so she assumed it was in good working order. But was it even loaded? She remembered his mocking reply when she'd asked: *There's one sure way to find out.*

There must be more than one way, Bernadette thought stubbornly as she slipped the light revolver out of its holster. She fiddled with it nervously, not knowing what she was looking for, exactly, only that there had to be some way to get the bullets *into* the damned thing. When the cylinder snapped free she nearly dropped the gun, believing she'd either broken it or that it was about to go off in her hands. Then she realised she was staring at six small chambers, and that each of them held a shiny new bullet.

She fumbled with the gun until the cylinder fell back in place, then sat back and passed a trembling hand over her forehead. How could he let her walk around for the last five days with a loaded gun pointed straight down at her foot? What if she'd tripped, or fallen, for God's sake! The very thought made her queasy, and she glared at Forrester, lying motionless a few feet away. He could have *told* her it was loaded, couldn't he? She'd never seriously considered it would be, as he'd very well known!

'Wake up, Sam,' she muttered under her breath. 'You've had your rest, you insufferable chauvinist! *You're* supposed to be taking care of *me*, remember?'

There was no reaction at all, not a muscle twitched. Bernadette wriggled back against his pack and settled down with a weary, dejected sigh. Not two seconds later a loud rustling in the brush behind her had her scrambling to Forrester's side on her knees in stark terror.

'Sam!' she hissed as she brought the gun from its holster and held it straight out in front of her in both hands.

'Sam, *please*! There's something prowling around out there!'

She glanced down at him, but he hadn't moved. Oh what was she supposed to do, now? If she fired the gun, the mercenaries might hear the shot and come running. And if she didn't, she might become lunch for some ravenous beast of the jungle.

'*Shoo!*' she cried in desperation. 'Scat, whatever you are! Scram! *Beat it*, do you hear!'

Clasping the gun in her left hand, she picked up a seed pod the size of her fist and threw it as hard as she could at the spot where the noise seemed to have originated. There was a snuffling grunt, and then the sounds of something beating a hasty retreat.

The pistol became a loathesome, repugnant thing as she realised how close she had come to actually firing it, and she wasted no time in getting it back into its holster. She gazed down at Forrester helplessly, silently beseeching him to open his eyes and say something, even if it was only one of his snide remarks. Wasn't he *ever* going to wake up?

'Sam?' she said softly, resting her palm on his cheek to check for fever. His skin was warm, but not unusually so. 'Please, Sam. I'm starting to get really scared, you big ox. Wake up, please.'

She waited. Nothing. Not even his breathing altered.

'Sam! Please wake up!' She grasped his shoulders and shook him, really worried now. 'Listen, Sam Forrester, don't you *dare* die on me! Wake up! Wake up, do you hear me!' Her voice rising, she drew back her hand and slapped him, hard.

He stirred and his eyelids flickered, then lifted to treat her to the sight of clear grey eyes, both pupils contracting normally as the light hit them.

'Bernie?' His voice was raspy as he blinked and then sat up.

'Oh, thank God!' she said fervently. 'How do you feel? Does your arm hurt much?'

'My arm?' He looked down at it, then frowned as he fingered the bandage. 'You wrecked the Jeep,' he said flatly.

Bernadette stiffened and her cheeks flamed. 'Yes, I wrecked the Jeep,' she snapped. 'And then I dragged you out of it and bandaged your precious arm, not that I expect any gratitude, mind you.'

Her sarcastic outburst left him unmoved. 'You did a nice job. Did you think to clean it first?'

'Of course I cleaned it first! What do you take me for, a complete idiot?' She scrambled to her feet, muttering something about ingrates under her breath, then marched to where his pack lay. Rummaging for his spare shirt, she didn't look around when he asked:

'What did you use?'

'That,' she answered curtly, flicking a hand at the bottle sitting beside her own pack.

There was a short, disbelieving silence, and then Forrester bawled, '*Whisky*! Bernie, are you telling me you used *whisky* to clean my arm!'

'Well, that's what they——' Her mouth suddenly snapped shut. She couldn't tell him that was what they always used in the movies.

'We've got an entire medical kit crammed full of antibiotics and antiseptics, and you poured George's cheap, rotgut whisky on an open wound! Terrific,' he growled. 'I'll be lucky if I don't die of blood poisoning. Wouldn't it have been simpler to just shoot me, or club me to death while I was unconscious?'

Bernadette jumped up and spun around to face him, her hands clenched on his shirt. She didn't know whether she was more hurt or angry, but she *did* know she wasn't about to take his abuse lying down.

'You know, I could really do without your insulting sarcasm,' she told him in a voice that only shook a little. 'I mean, I did my best. I did all I knew how to do, without your help or expert advice. I got us *and* our gear off the road and under cover, which in itself ought to earn me some kind of weightlifting medal. Then I sat here with a gun I didn't know how to use, for what seemed like hours, prepared to protect you from . . . from whatever you needed protecting from, not knowing when you'd come to or even *if* you would, and . . . and this is the thanks I get!' She drew a jerky breath, pride driving her to conceal her hurt with angry words. 'Let me tell you something, *Colonel* Forrester—I think if I had it all to do over again, I'd take my chances on Claude's airplane. *You* are positively the most foul-tempered, pig-headed, totally insensitive individual I've ever had the misfortune to meet!'

She ended the speech by turning smartly on her heel and stalking off, her back as stiff and straight as a poker and her small fists clutching his shirt. Tears blurred her vision, but she'd have blundered into a herd of rhinos before she'd lift a hand to wipe them away. She eventually halted and tried to get a grip on herself, determined not to go back until she was fully in control.

Forrester moved so quietly that she didn't know he was there until his gruff voice came from behind her.

'I'm sorry,' he murmured. 'What I said ... I didn't mean it, Bernie.'

It was the last straw. Her frayed nerves started to unravel, and the tears she'd managed to bring under control gushed from her eyes and coursed down her pale cheeks. Bernadette shook her head helplessly, knowing her voice would give her away. She gulped to swallow the lump in her throat and heard his heavy sigh.

'I was angry,' he said in quiet explanation.

'No kidding.' The sarcastic comment slipped out despite her resolve to remain silent, and when he heard the thickness of her voice he laid a hand on her shoulder.

'Bernie? Are you crying?' He sounded surprised.

She shook her head vehemently and stepped out from under his hand. He sighed again.

'I wasn't angry at *you*,' he muttered impatiently. 'It was the situation I found myself in when I came to. I felt ... vulnerable.'

The admission touched her, because she could guess what it had cost him to make. A warm glow began to spread through her, banishing the hurt his insensitivity had caused. He waited a moment, and when she didn't respond he asked quietly: 'Could I have my shirt?'

Bernadette hadn't been aware she was still holding it.

She thrust it behind her with one hand, wishing he'd go away so she could mop up her face and regain her dignity before she faced him again. Futile hope. His lean fingers fastened around her arm to turn her, gently but firmly. When she ducked her head, his other hand came up to lift her chin.

'Bernie!'

She took the soft exclamation as criticism, and her chin firmed up in his hand.

'Well, what did you expect? I have feelings, too,' she said huskily.

Forrester's eyes clouded as he framed her face in both his hands, his slender fingers gently wiping away her tears.

'I never doubted it,' he said gravely. 'Forgive me, Bernadette? Even if I don't deserve it?'

It was the first time he'd spoken her name correctly, and hearing it sent a wave of foolish, giddy pleasure through her. She nodded willingly as she looked into his sombre eyes.

'Okay.'

He smiled, and her heart turned over. 'That was easy.'

As he looked deep into her eyes, Bernadette stood quietly, acutely conscious that he hadn't removed his hands. They rested lightly on her flushed cheeks, his palms cool and hard, his touch unbelievably gentle.

'Did you really stand guard over me with a gun?' he asked, something like wonder shading his voice and darkening his eyes.

Bernadette moved her head in affirmation. She suddenly felt too short of breath to attempt speech, and she was finding it all but impossible to remember she was supposed to be a nun. His bare, muscular chest was only inches away. All she had to do was to lift her own hands, and . . .

His head began a slow descent, and her heart knocked against her ribs, her breath staggering on the way to her lungs. She stood absolutely still; otherwise she'd have probably shocked him right out of his mind. Then again, maybe not, she thought with a touch of nervous hysteria. She watched the approach of his lips like someone in a trance, imagining what they would feel like on hers. Her eyes closed in sweet anticipation, and then she felt his mouth brush her forehead softly.

'You never cease to amaze me,' Sam murmured, stepping away to pull on his shirt. He finished buttoning it, then asked absently, 'Where are my specs?'

'In your pack.' If he noticed the hoarseness in her voice, he gave no indication. He merely nodded, favouring his left arm slightly as he shrugged into the pack. 'We'd better move out,' he said as he tossed hers to her.

Bernadette's disappointment was quickly replaced by concern for him. 'Shouldn't you rest a while? You could have a concussion, and your arm——'

'From the feel of my head, I'd say the concussion's a certainty,' Forrester agreed, his tone dry. 'A mild one, anyway. But my arm's fine. It's only a flesh wound.' His sudden grin surprised her. 'I've always wanted to be able to say that.'

He hefted the rifle and took a moment to reload it, then gestured for her to follow as he started off into the bush, heading away from the road.

Despite his claims to the contrary, Bernadette could tell he was tiring as the day wore on. A concussion— even a mild one—was nothing to sneeze at, and even if his arm wasn't bleeding, it had to be sore as hell. Her tentative suggestion that they stop for a rest was curtly rebuffed, and she made up her mind not to say another word as she tramped along behind him, frowning at the spreading dark patch between his shoulder blades. Stubborn, mule-headed cuss!

It was only midafternoon when he called a halt and slipped out of his pack. The slow, careful way Sam moved his arms and powerful shoulders was evidence of his pain and exhaustion, but still he took the rifle and made a reconnaissance of the area before allowing Bernadette to divest herself of her pack.

'God, I'm beat,' he muttered as he eased himself to the ground. 'George is right, I'm getting too old for this kind of thing. Bring me that bottle, will you?'

Bernadette didn't speak as she removed the whisky from her pack and carried it to him. She sat beside him, examining his hard-boned face with affectionate concern. She would never have wished him ill, but she had to admit he was much easier to take, now that he'd been forced to an acceptance of his own limitations, his own mortality. Still, she sensed that admitting he wasn't as impervious as he'd always believed was particularly hard for him.

'So far today, you've taken part in a bar-room brawl, been shot, had the Jeep you were a passenger in rammed into a tree, and then hiked about fifteen miles,' she recited quietly. 'You're suffering from concussion and blood loss, and you've driven yourself to the point of collapse.' She paused to shrug. 'But aside from those few minor difficulties, I fail to see why you should be tired. Maybe you *are* getting old. I'll bet what you need is a good tonic.'

She held out the bottle, and a slow grin transformed Sam's grim mouth as he accepted it. He was really something when he grinned like that, let the wicked little boy inside peep out for a moment.

'Sister, you are a woman after my own heart,' he drawled. He uncapped the bottle, then offered it to her. 'Join me?'

Bernadette refused with a smiling shake of her head. 'I don't think so, thanks.'

'Come on,' he coaxed, the grin still in evidence. 'One teensy little nip won't hurt. I guarantee it beats the rusty water I got from Aggie's pump.'

Against her better judgment, Bernadette let herself be convinced. She was by no means a teetotaller, but the whisky she was accustomed to was smooth and mellow, having been aged in oaken barrels for several years. She doubted this stuff had ever seen the inside of a barrel as it scorched a path to her stomach.

Forrester watched her closely, frowning in disappointment when she didn't choke. Bernadette handed the bottle back to him and tried to hide her amusement.

'It's rather strong. Does George make it himself?'

'No.' Forrester was still frowning as he tipped the bottle to his mouth. 'There's a family of natives who've been brewing the stuff for years. They won't give away the recipe, but they sell it to him for next to nothing. George provides the empty bottles. One time it might be labelled Scotch, the next time gin or vodka.' He offered the bottle again, challenging her with his eyes as he murmured, 'Have another drink to wash the dust from your mouth.'

Bernadette had never been able to resist a dare. She accepted the bottle and deliberately took a long swallow of the potent liquor while he watched, his frown growing deeper by the second.

Neither of them stopped to consider that they hadn't eaten since breakfast, and in a remarkably short time the contents of the bottle had been reduced by half. Bernadette was feeling just a little tipsy, warm and fuzzy-headed as she partially reclined against Forrester's pack, sharing it with him as a backrest.

'You are the damnedest woman,' he remarked for perhaps the tenth time since he'd met her. He held the bottle in front of his face, squinting at it. 'Why on earth aren't you unconscious?'

Bernadette smiled dreamily at the confused amazement in his voice. 'Must be my metabolism,' she murmured on a sigh. 'Some people get drunk just sniffing a bar towel, and others can consume extraordinary amounts of alcohol and remain perfectly sober. At least, that's what I've heard.'

'But a *nun*? A *nun*! Nuns don't even drink, do they?'

'Not usually, no,' Bernadette answered, then squirmed around to face him, giving in to the sudden urge to do a little teasing of her own. 'You seem to possess a lot of preconceived, prejudicial ideas about nuns, Colonel'

He snorted. 'A lot of *inaccurate* ideas, if you're anything to go by. You are the damnedest——'

'Woman. I know. You've already expressed that opinion once or twice.' She sat up to run a hand through her short hair, then stretched and yawned, pulling the fabric of her shirt taut over her high, firm breasts. 'Isn't it about suppertime?'

Forrester watched her through narrowed eyes, a disturbingly sensual smile hovering around his mouth. One knee was bent, and the hand holding the bottle dangled over it carelessly.

'Are you hungry?'

His slow, husky drawl raised goosebumps on Bernadette's arms and made her stomach muscles quiver, then clench. 'No, but I think we ought to——'

'Neither am I. Not for food, anyway. So why bother? Come here,' as he lifted his injured arm and beckoned with his fingers.

Bernadette eyed him nervously, afraid of what she saw in his smoky eyes, but more afraid of her own immediate, powerful response to that look. 'What do you mean "come here"?'

'Just what I said,' he drawled. His hand suddenly captured her wrist and he tugged. Caught off balance, Bernadette fell against his chest, and was held there by the arm which immediately locked around her.

'Colonel!'

'What happened to Sam?' he mocked lazily.

'I might ask you the same question! Let me up!'

But when she pushed against his chest, his arm contracted to hold her in place.

'Keep that up and you'll start my wound bleeding again,' he warned softly.

Bernadette ceased struggling at once, knowing he had her trapped and irritated by the knowledge.

'What, exactly, do you think you're doing?' she demanded coldly, desperate not to let him know how he was affecting her. 'If this is your idea of a joke——'

'Oh, shut up.' The exasperated mutter halted her midsentence, and she stared at him in surprise. He drew a deep breath, then released it slowly. 'I'm not going to attack you, Bernadette. I just want to feel a warm human body next to me for a while, that's all. Can't you forget you're a nun for ten minutes and relax?'

She could hardly tell him the reason she couldn't relax was that it would be all too easy to forget she was *supposed* to be a nun, with his arms around her and his warm human body pressed intimately against her warm human body.

'You promise you won't——'

'Trust me,' Sam said soberly, his eyes holding hers as he

eased her on to his chest, shifting her weight off his arm.

Bernadette settled down against him, but she was far from comfortable. She lay tense and silent, not daring to move for fear she'd bring them into even closer contact.

'Tell me what you thought of Belfast,' he murmured after a while.

Bernadette hesitated. 'What do you mean? What I thought of it, how?'

'What colour do you remember it as?'

It didn't occur to her to consider the question strange. She knew what he meant: certain places, or sometimes people, presented themselves to the subconscious as colours, or shapes, or textures. All the many impressions they made mingled and blended to form one sense memory, which lingered vividly long after the individual details had faded from recollection.

'When I first arrived, I saw the city and the people in it as grey,' she answered quietly. 'Grey everywhere. Grey buildings, grey streets, grey children in grey clothes.'

Sam's bearded cheek brushed her forehead as he nodded. 'And when you left? What colour was it, then?'

Bernadette didn't hesitate over her answer. 'Red,' she whispered, remembering the young bomb victims she'd seen carried into the hospital, their clothing saturated, dripping blood on to the green tile floor to form an obscene mosaic. She shivered involuntarily, and felt Forrester's arm press against her ribs in response.

'That's how I remember it, too,' he said softly. 'I don't guess I'll ever be able to think of Belfast without associating it with the colour red.'

Bernadette closed her eyes and impulsively slipped her arm around his waist, seeking the comfort of his warmth. 'Could we please talk about something else?' she asked, her voice strained.

'Sure.' He gave her another gentle squeeze, which she accepted gratefully. 'What's your favourite food?'

'In all the world?' she asked as she tipped her head back with a smile.

'In all the whole wide world. If you could have anything you wanted to eat, right now, this minute, what would it be?'

She bit her lip in indecision, then answered, 'Apples. Any kind. Red or Golden Delicious, or Winesaps, or even the sour green ones that grow on an old, gnarled tree in my grandmother's back yard. I'd love to sink my teeth into a crisp, cold apple ... let the juice run down my chin, and munch it all the way to the core. How about you?' she asked as Sam grinned down at her. 'What's your favourite food in all the world?'

He laughed, and it was a warm, lovely sound, rumbling up from his chest and filling her head with the sound of violins.

'Pecan pie,' he answered with another grin. 'The kind they serve down south, made with real butter and lots of great big pecans.'

'Down south?' Bernadette repeated in surprise. 'You mean ... down *South*, like in the States, down South?'

'Mmhmm. Like New Orleans or Charleston.'

'You've been there?' She was amazed.

'Yes, I've been there,' he drawled humorously. 'I've been to a lot of places, many of which I don't care to remember.'

Bernadette shook her head in wonder as she nestled back against his chest. 'You never cease to amaze me,' she murmured wryly, and his amused chuckle vibrated in her ear.

She waited a while, and then, because he seemed so relaxed and open, more approachable than he'd ever been, she asked softly:

'Sam, will you tell me about your parents?'

He was silent for so long that she was afraid she'd made him withdraw again; close up on her, shut her out. Bernadette was disappointed and hurt that he didn't trust her enough to let her share what she sensed was a personal tragedy. She tilted her head on his shoulder to look up at him, her voice low and husky as she murmured:

'I'm sorry, I shouldn't have asked.'

'No. It's all right.' Sam's eyes met hers, a sad smile in their depths. And then he rested his head against his pack, staring straight up, beyond the trees, beyond the sky, to a time and place known only to him. Bernadette's arm curved more closely at his waist in a protective, purely instinctive gesture as she waited.

'My father was what I guess you'd call a diplomat,' he began quietly. 'At any rate, he was attached to the Foreign Office and we moved around a lot, all over Africa. He always referred to himself as a civil servant. I suspected there was more to it than he let on—that his duties went beyond filling out forms and attending Embassy functions, that sort of thing—though of course I couldn't be sure.' He frowned for a moment, absorbed by his own thoughts, then went on.

'Anyway, he supposedly "retired" when I was fifteen. We continued to live in Kenya, though. It was home to us by then, and even with the unrest there at the time, we didn't want to leave.' A harsh note entered his gravelly voice as he said, 'If we had, both my parents would still be alive. I came home from school one day and discovered them. They'd both been——' He cut himself off abruptly, his head swivelling towards Bernadette. She was helpless to conceal the horror and shock she felt, her imagination running rampant.

'Oh, Sam!' she whispered thickly, aching for him, for the boy he had been. 'I'm sorry. I'm so sorry.' She took a moment to regain control of her voice, then asked, 'What did you do? Where did you go? You said you didn't have any other family.'

'That wasn't strictly true,' he murmured, his voice flat and unemotional. 'There was an elderly aunt in England—my mother's sister. I was sent to her to finish my schooling. We made each other thoroughly miserable while I was with her,' he added with a wry twist of his mouth. 'As soon as I was old enough, I enlisted in the army, but I always knew I'd end up back here, someday.'

'Why?' Bernadette asked softly. 'When you retired, why did you come back to Africa—why not settle in England?'

His light shrug was negligent. 'There was nothing for me there. I didn't belong. And once you've lived here, seen all this, breathed the air,' he waved the bottle of whisky in a gesture that encompassed their immediate surroundings and everything beyond, 'it's in your blood. A man can be free here, like nowhere else. You feel a part of nature. Even if you live and work in concrete buildings in the middle of a city, you're always aware that a few short hours away another world exists—a world you can escape to, breathe free in, away from hypocrisy and man's inhumanity to man. It's just you and the elements . . . and God, of course,' he added with a teasing grin.

'So you do believe in God,' Bernadette said huskily.

She had been deeply moved by all he'd said, by the glimpse he'd allowed her of the self he usually took such pains to conceal from the rest of the world. Never again would she think of him as hard or unfeeling. Callous, yes, and cynical, but wasn't that to be expected, after all he'd seen, all he'd suffered? She had already come to respect him during the last few days; now that respect was doubled, tripled. She would always be grateful that she'd been given the opportunity to meet him.

Sam's grin turned mocking. 'The question is, does He believe in me?' he drawled. 'What do you think, Sister?'

Bernadette smiled up at him. 'Oh, yes. You might try His patience from time to time, but I suspect that overall He's rather pleased with the way you've turned out, Colonel.'

He merely gave her a surprised look, his head cocked to one side, and then chuckled softly as he settled back against his pack.

They lay without speaking, both content to just share the 'peace and the companionable silence. Bernadette slipped into a state of drowsy half-awareness, and the first time she felt his lips at her temple she didn't move or make a protest. Then his fingers began to slowly caress her arm and they returned, parted this time, his warm breath stirring her hair. She sighed and reluctantly roused herself to complain.

'Sam, don't, please. You shouldn't.'

'I know,' he sighed, sounding regretful. 'I've spent the better part of the last week watching you, and listening to your voice, and spreading my bedroll next to yours at night, and in all that time I've been a good boy and kept my hands to myself. But dammit, Bernie, I'm only human,' he growled. 'I can't spend every waking hour reminding myself you're a nun. God help me, I can't even *think* of you as a nun most of the time. All I *can* think of when I look at you is what I've seen of that beautiful body, and how it felt when I held you in my arms and kissed your mouth.'

Bernadette felt like she was drowning. His rough voice, the tormenting caress of his hand, his hard, warm body, all worked together to undermine her willpower and rouse needs and wants she'd rather remained dormant.

'Don't,' she begged softly. 'Don't think of those things!'

His laugh was harsh and humourless. 'You think I *want* to think of them? I'm not into self-abuse, Bernie. I try not to think of you at all, but every time I turn my head, there you are, within easy reach, and sometimes it's all I can do to keep from dragging you to the ground and ripping your clothes off.'

Bernadette shook her head, her eyes closed tight. The vision he conjured up was far too dangerous for her peace of mind. The thought of him taking her—roughly, even brutally—terrified her, because she suspected she would welcome it, glory in it, in fact. And she wasn't ready to face that side of herself yet, much less deal with it.

'Sam, please!' she whispered, but he ignored the plea.

'And don't tell me to pray,' he muttered savagely. 'If I pray for anything, it sure won't be for restraint! Shall I tell you what I'd like to pray for, Sister?' he murmured against her skin as he mouthed the tender area at her temple.

'No,' she moaned, her resistance dwindling fast.

'You don't want to know?' he taunted softly. 'But, Sister, confession is supposed to be good for the soul, and you *are* concerned for my soul, aren't you?'

At the moment she was more concerned for her own sanity. 'You promised!' she gasped as his lips left a trail of sultry kisses down the side of her face. 'You said to trust you!'

'Ah, but how can you trust me,' he whispered as his mouth closed in, moist and warm and almost impossible to resist, 'when I can't even trust myself? Oh God, Bernie, I *want* you!'

CHAPTER NINE

THE last sentence was as tormented as his kiss. His open mouth plundered and ravaged, but Bernadette sensed that the pain he was inflicting was nothing compared to the self-loathing he felt. She instinctively lifted a hand to his head, stroking his hair with a gentle, soothing touch. The action seemed to drain the anger from him. His lips softened, then pulled away briefly before returning to sip delicately at hers.

The change in tactics was Bernadette's undoing. Where his frustration and pain had elicited compassion, this slow, tender lovemaking made her ache for more. Her lips parted on a silent moan, her fingers slowly threading through his hair.

Forrester felt her unwilling response, of course. He pulled back fractionally to look into her eyes, saw the struggle there, the uncertainty and doubt. But he also saw the growing desire she was powerless to conceal. His eyes glittered with awareness as his fingers trailed up her arm to her neck, and then around to the nape.

His mouth quirked in a cynical smile as he glanced at the bottle of whisky, then set it aside to wrap both arms around her. His nimble fingers dealt with the buttons of her shirt in short order, then the flimsy barrier of her bra was impatiently pushed up over her breasts, laying them bare for his lips and tongue.

Bernadette's head twisted from side to side as she fought to retain even a modicum of control. Oh, how he knew how to do that! Her jaw clenched to contain a groan as strong white teeth closed with exquisite care on a nipple and a rough tongue flicked and teased it to excruciating arousal.

He lifted his head, his chest rising and falling heavily with his disturbed breathing. 'Touch me,' he asked, not satisfied with her passive acceptance. He took her hands and placed them on his shirt in encouragement, and though Bernadette tried to hold them still, her fingers began to fumble agitatedly with his buttons. Tears filled her eyes as she felt her very will disintegrating. She shook her head desperately, snatching her hands away in a last-ditch effort to regain control.

'I can't,' she whispered brokenly. 'Please, Sam. I can't.'

'Yes, you can,' he murmured, his voice husky. His own hands finished what hers had started, exposing his chest to her gaze. 'You want me, too,' he muttered, and the catch in his voice told her how uncertain his own control was. 'I can see it in your eyes, and feel it in the way you tremble against me, and hear it in the way your breath jerks against your throat.'

He closed his eyes as he brought her hands back to him, sliding them inside his shirt, placing them at his lean waist. She could feel the taut, economical way his skin stretched over his ribs, warm and damp under her palms. Her fingers spread, once more overriding her will, and his stomach contracted in reaction, the long muscles of his thighs tensing against hers.

'*Yes*,' he moaned softly. 'Oh, oh, yes, Bernie. Please.'

The husky plea was all the encouragement her wayward hands needed. They glided around to his back, luxuriating in the spasmodic welcome they received, then skimmed his ribcage to traverse the breadth of his lightly furred, beautifully formed chest, pausing briefly to tweak a hair here or examine an erect nipple there, then finally slid purposefully up to link at the back of his neck.

Sam released a long, shuddering breath and lowered himself to her, supporting his weight on his elbows as he clasped her head between his hands to kiss her deeply. Her breasts flattened against his chest and she felt him insinuate himself between her thighs, slowly, so as not to alarm her. And then he began to move, his pelvis gyrating with careful restraint. His hardness hurt as he ground her hips beneath his, and Bernadette squirmed to try and ease the pressure. She realised her mistake when Sam groaned into her mouth and his already passionate kiss became a frenzied attempt to devour her, sending her senses reeling.

'Bernadette!' he gasped, wrenching his mouth from hers, pressing it to the side of her throat. His breath was coming hard, and he seemed to find speech difficult.

'Bernie...can't you tell, don't you know—?' He caught himself, his hands gentling as they moved through her hair. 'No, of course you don't,' he breathed into her ear. 'I want you to be ready, to know what to expect. When I move, move with me, but smoothly, matching my rhythm. Like this.'

His hands shifted to her hips, demonstrating until her body instinctively took over and they were freed to begin a leisurely exploration of the rest of her soft, yielding body.

Bernadette was an apt and willing pupil. She exercised her newly mastered skill with an eager abandon that had him shuddering in helpless response.

'Oh, Bernie,' he half laughed, half groaned as her slender legs twined around his and her hands slipped low on his back to urge him even closer. 'Sweet Bernie, you're incredible! You see?' he murmured, smiling down at her. 'There's nothing to it. And it's good, isn't it?'

'Yes,' she whispered breathlessly as she clutched at him. 'Good. But not enough. Please, Sam ... more.'

She could see that she'd shocked him, but she was beyond caring. From the moment she touched his naked flesh, she had been committed. Away with this idiotic charade! It had been doomed to failure from the start. She must have been out of her mind to think she'd be able to carry it off—passing herself off as a *nun*, for heaven's sake!

She'd abandoned all pretence the moment she accepted the fact that he was going to make love to her. It was inevitable, she realised now, had been from the beginning. The very first time they met, when he had literally dragged her out of a sleazy bar and into an alley, she had recognised him as something totally new to her experience, a force to be reckoned with. He was right: she did want him, more than she could ever have believed she'd want a man. He released something elemental in her, some primitive force she hadn't even been aware of until he came along. It was frightening, in a way, but it was also exhilarating and incredibly exciting. And the jungle, steamy and fraught with hidden dangers, seemed the perfect setting for their coming together. Her eyes heavy-lidded and hazy with desire, she wrapped herself around him, arching her body wantonly to his.

'Bernie,' Sam murmured, his voice rough as he stared down at her in astonished wonder. 'Oh, Bernie!' His mouth covered hers again, open and hot, slanting across her lips in hungry demand as his hand found the snap of her jeans.

'We may only have a few days, but I promise we'll make the most of them, sweetheart,' he muttered into her mouth.

The hoarse words hit her like a bucket of icewater, dousing her passion so effectively it might never have existed. He didn't seem to notice the way her muscles suddenly tensed and she went rigid in his embrace; or if he did, he must have mistaken the reaction as some sort of impassioned convulsion, a spasm of desire.

Only a few days. And two or three nights. And that was it—after that they'd go their separate ways, likely never to meet again.

Yet, knowing that—and still believing she was a nun!—he was prepared to take his pleasure with her while he could no matter what the consequences. Bernadette was filled with such an immense rage that for a moment she actually forgot she *wasn't* a nun. How *dare* he! The selfish, arrogant, self-centred *ass*!

His lean fingers brushed the softness of her stomach, then slipped under the elastic waist of her panties, and she sucked in her breath on a strangled gasp. He apparently believed she was only exhibiting virginal modesty, because he murmured rough words of reassurance in her ear while his long, cool fingers deliberately stroked their way downward.

'Stop it! No!' She was nearly incoherent with rage as she shoved at his chest.

'It's all right,' Sam coaxed in a sexy whisper. 'It's all right, Bernie. Just relax. I won't hurt you, sweetheart.'

'You're right, you won't,' she gritted under her breath, and heaved at him again.

He lifted his head slightly, his eyes glazed and slow to focus. 'What?' His broad forehead puckered, and he sounded distracted. Small wonder, Bernadette thought scornfully.

'Get off me! Sam, I mean it!' She wedged her arms between them and glared into his face, mere inches from hers. His frown deepened, but he didn't budge.

'There's no need to be afraid,' he murmured huskily. 'I swear, Bernie, I'll be——'

'I'm not afraid,' she hissed into his face. 'I just want you *off* me. *Now!*'

Forrester's jaw tensed and a steely look came into his eyes. 'Changed your mind, have you? Just like that?' His voice was dangerously soft, but Bernadette wasn't in the least intimidated.

'That's right! Just like that!' she snapped.

'Why?' he demanded, his eyes narrowing. 'You're not a tease, and I don't believe you are afraid.' He stared at her silently for a moment, his mind working with methodical precision behind those smoky grey eyes, and then his lips twisted in a cynical sneer. 'Experimenting, were you? Is that it? Using me to satisfy your curiosity?'

At that moment Bernadette actively hated him. She hated his mocking cynicism, and his arrogance, and his strutting chauvinism, but most of all she hated him for being willing to believe that she could and would lead a man on for such a shallow, self-serving purpose. At least now she knew what he really thought of her!

She held his eyes as she replied coldly: 'If that's what you choose to think, far be it from me to disillusion you, Colonel.'

The line of his mouth went hard with anger as his hands tightened in a cruel grip. 'You tease,' he snarled. 'All right, then, let's just satisfy this pathetic curiosity of yours. Put all your unanswered questions and pure-minded little fantasies to rest once and for all.'

Bernadette looked into his savage face and was

suddenly afraid. 'No,' she said in a throaty voice. 'Sam, don't.'

He ignored her, his kiss a punishment as he ground her lips back against her teeth. 'You might have changed your mind, *Sister*,'—he sneered the word in vicious contempt—'but I haven't. I still want you, and now I'll have you.'

He ignored her, his kiss a punishment as he ground desperate strength to her limbs as she began to fight him. How often had she read that no woman could be raped if she made up her mind not to be? But, oh, he was so strong! She used every weapon she possessed—knees and elbows, fists, fingernails, even her teeth when he pressed a shoulder on to her collarbone to hold her in place while he yanked ruthlessly at her clothes.

'Stay still! You vicious little cat!' he growled when her white teeth sank into his flesh and she had the intense satisfaction of tasting his blood in her mouth.

She took advantage of his surprise to seize a handful of his hair, then did her level best to rip it out of his scalp as she levered his head back away from her. Sam was forced to abandon his attempts to strip her in order to defend himself. His hand flew up to grasp her wrist, but she refused to relinquish her grip on his hair. The best he could manage was to immobilise her hand so she couldn't snatch him bald. In the meantime his other hand captured her left wrist and pinned it over her head. He raised himself above her, breathing hard, his eyes glittering with sexual excitement.

'Give it up, Bernie,' he growled between laboured breaths.

'Never!' she spat, and then suddenly twisted her leg beneath his and jerked her knee up towards his groin.

'No you don't!' he muttered as he narrowly avoided the well-aimed blow. 'You little hellion! Stop it, Bernie!' he ordered as she struggled to wrench her hands free. 'I said stop it!'

'*Pig!*' she flung at him venomously, her eyes spitting furious defiance. He had to tighten his grip on her left wrist to hold her, and she felt the skin pinch as she tried to twist her arm free.

'You're only going to hurt yourself,' he warned, his brow furrowed in an infuriating pretence at concern.

'I'd rather hurt *you*!' Bernadette panted, and tried to bring her knee up again, but he trapped her leg under his and foiled the attempt.

Forrester's mouth slanted in wry mockery. 'You already are, or hadn't you noticed?' he drawled. The significance of the remark wasn't lost on her, and her cheeks flamed. It was obvious that her struggles were only increasing his desire, and she found the fact utterly disgusting.

'You filthy animal!' she choked in uncontrolled fury.

His amused grin left her nearly catatonic with rage, and a spurt of adrenalin combined with the slight lowering of his guard enabled her to yank her left arm free. Her fingers hooked like talons, she raked her nails down the side of his face, leaving four deep scratches, and the instant she felt his grip on her right arm slacken, she freed it, as well.

Sam's hand went to his cheek in stunned disbelief, and, putting everything she had into her arms, Bernadette shoved against his chest. He was caught off balance, allowing her to roll out from under him, but before she could scramble to her feet he recaptured her from behind. As he tried to confine her arms, she jabbed backwards with an elbow, and heard his soft grunt of pain when she connected with his ribcage.

'Dammit, Bernie, don't make me hurt you,' he grated in her ear, trying without much success to capture her arms and at the same time hold her clamped against him.

'You're going to have to,' she panted in grim determination. 'You're going to have to knock me out, at the very least, because the *only* way you'll have me is if I'm unconscious!'

While they wrestled on their knees, she managed to refasten her jeans and tug her bra back down. Her appearance at least partially restored to normal, she turned her attention to doing as much damage to him as she could in the hope that if she caused him enough pain he might decide raping her wasn't worth the effort.

His left arm was hooked around her waist, and she dug her nails into the back of his hand, where there was vitually nothing to cushion the nerves and bones. His hissing breath was followed by a muttered curse, and then he abruptly stood up, dragging her with him, holding her clear of the ground as he yanked her hand away.

He soon realised what a serious tactical error he'd made. Her feet were now free to kick back at his shins while her curled fingers twisted and clawed at the air, trying to get just one good swipe at a bare patch of skin.

'Ouch!' he muttered as she suddenly threw her head back, hoping to crack his skull open, no doubt.

The spitting, clawing, biting bundle of fury he held prisoner only by the sheer superiority of his strength had him dumbfounded with amazement. Could this be the same cool, self-contained little schoolteacher-nun he'd spent the last several days with?

Her heel delivered another vicious kick to his shin, and he winced. She was a fighter! He must be double her weight, and she had to know she couldn't win. All he had to do was wait for her to wear herself out. His mouth tilted in a wry grin, which Bernadette thankfully couldn't see. Of course, by then he would most likely be bloody well exhausted, himself. Was that what she was counting on?

If she'd only known it, she'd never been in danger of being raped. Angered and frustrated, he'd only meant to throw a scare into her, punish her a bit in retaliation. He readily accepted the blame for the entire mess, not that it did him a whole lot of good. He never should have consumed so much of George's cheap whisky. or egged her on after her first drink. It was just that he couldn't believe it when she downed the stuff like it was tea with honey and lemon. The woman was absolutely incredible! He'd never known anyone like her in his life, and probably never would again.

He *liked* her, he realised with no small amount of amazement. He liked her a lot, and it was an unfamiliar experience for him, to feel that way about a woman. Of course he also lusted after her, but that suddenly seemed to decrease in importance as he savoured the other sensation for the first time. He looked down at her, an odd, quirking smile on his lips as she squirmed against his hold, and thought one more time that she was the damnedest woman he'd ever met.

'Bernie, settle down,' he said in a calm, reasonable tone, and got an elbow in his ribs in reply. 'Bernie, I said settle down!' he growled, shifting his grip to pin her arms to her sides. 'I'm not going to——'

'You bet your *life* you're not, Buster!' she gritted through her teeth, and an irrepressible grin spread over Sam's face. 'Not while I've got breath left in my body!'

He decided she probably wouldn't believe he meant her no harm as long as he was holding her against her will. He carefully lowered her to the ground, his arms falling away in a gesture of goodwill, and she promptly spun around and brought her left fist up to deliver a glancing blow to his chin.

He almost hit her back before he caught himself. His eyebrows drew together over the bridge of his nose and he lifted a hand to rub at his jaw, muttering, 'What did you do that for?' as he took a step towards her.

'Stay away from me!' Bernadette ordered, retreating and grappling with the buttons of her shirt at the same time. 'I mean it! If you touch me again, I'll—I'll——'

'You'll what?' Sam mocked softly. He folded his arms over his chest and braced his feet apart, enjoying her confusion as she eyed him suspiciously. She couldn't figure out why he'd let her go, and it was clear she didn't trust him an inch.

Bernadette rubbed her damp palms on the legs of her jeans in agitation, and the side of her right hand bumped against the holster. Without thinking, she snatched the pistol free in panic-inspired haste for the second time that day, once more holding it in front of her in a stiff-armed, two-hand grip.

Forrester tensed, but didn't move. The situation was no longer in the least amusing. He recognised the desperate look in her eyes, the terrified quaking of her body, and cursed himself for the worst kind of bloody damned fool. His stupid male pride had brought them to this; that, and the need to punish her, frighten her a little. Well, he'd certainly succeeded, far beyond his idiotic, juvenile intent.

'Bernie,' he said quietly. 'Put the gun away.'

Her head jerked in denial. 'No,' she refused, her voice quavering.

'Listen,' he began, injecting all the sincerity he could muster into his voice, but she shook her head again, keeping the bore of the pistol pointed in the general direction of his upper torso.

'No, *you* listen!' She sucked in a tortured breath, her voice rising now, approaching hysteria, and Sam judiciously fell silent.

'I know you think I was ... leading you on ... teasing you, but ... but it's not true! There's a name for women who ... who are like that, and I'm not one of them! I'm *not*! I never intended—I'm sorry, I'm truly sorry, but I never meant for what happened to happen. I swear I didn't!'

She'd started to cry, huge tears rolling down her pale cheeks. She paused to sniffle and gulp, then drew another ragged breath. When she spoke again, her voice was stronger, with a determination that caused his eyes to narrow.

'But I won't let you take me like some animal. I *won't*, Sam, do you understand? Whatever I have to do to stop you, I'll do.'

He didn't doubt her for a second. She felt backed to the wall, cornered, and in such a position she could be capable of just about anything. He wasn't afraid, but he did possess a healthy amount of respect for the gun she had levelled at his breastbone. He had to get the thing away from her, and he had to do it without hurting her. That was his only immediate goal; explanations and apologies could come later—if she'd listen to them, he thought wryly.

'Bernadette,' he began quietly as he started to advance on her, taking slow, nonthreatening steps, 'we both know you won't shoot me. You couldn't. So why don't you just——'

Her mouth twisted and a sob was wrenched from her throat. 'Oh, you know me so well, don't you?' she cried bitterly. 'You're right, of course. I couldn't shoot you. But maybe I could——' She suddenly lifted the gun, placing the muzzle against her right temple and holding it there with her trembling left hand.

'Bernie, *no!*'

Sam's hand shot out in reflexive horror, and her grip tightened, her finger curling around the trigger.

'Don't try it!' she said in a thick but steady voice.

He froze, his fingers curling into his palms. Now he *was* afraid. Dear God, how had this happened? He felt like he was living a nightmare. His fear made him angry, and he deliberately focused on the anger, welcoming it, letting it fill him, until the fear was overshadowed by it.

'Stop behaving like a bloody lunatic and put the bloody gun away!' he ordered furiously. *'Now!'*

Bernadette blinked in frowning uncertainty. When he sensed that her determination was weakening, he leaped at her, wrenching the pistol out of her unresisting grip. He was *shaking*, he realised in angry amazement, while she just stood there and stared at him with huge, blank eyes.

'You *stupid* little fool!' he raged. 'I ought to beat the living daylights out of you!'

Bernadette jerked in reaction, her head coming up. 'I think I'd prefer that to what you were trying to do ten minutes ago,' she told him with acid bitterness.

Sam's neck turned a dull shade of brick red, and then the colour swept up under his beard and on to his high cheekbones.

'I wasn't going to do anything,' he growled, then made an impatient gesture with his hand. 'At least, not what you thought.'

Her expression was one of outright disbelief, her eyes boring holes in him and making him want to squirm.

'You said,' she began in accusation, '. . . you said you still . . . wanted me,'—her voice wobbled over the last two words—'and that you'd have me. That's exactly what you said, and then—'

'You don't have to recite the whole bloody thing from memory,' Sam muttered. 'I know what I said, *and* what I did! But I've never forced myself on a woman in my life, and I had no intention of starting with you. I only intended to frighten you a little, just enough to teach you a lesson.'

He would have said more, but the resounding crack when her open hand struck his cheek cut him off and jerked his head to one side.

'Teach me a lesson!' she echoed in trembling, breathless rage. 'You were trying to teach me a *lesson*! Frighten me *a little bit*!'

She suddenly broke off, clutching at her chest. She had turned a ghastly shade of white, and she was trembling from head to foot, apparently having difficulty breathing, her delicate features contorted with the effort.

'Bernie!'

Forrester's hand closed on her upper arm in anxious concern, but she flinched away, her mouth twisting in fear.

'Don't!' Bernadette managed to gasp. 'Don't touch me!'

She was badly frightened, because she didn't know what was happening to her. She seemed to have lost all control of her body; her limbs were trembling violently and starting to go numb, and it was a tortured struggle to draw air into her starving lungs, but even more terrifying was the frantic, sledgehammer beat of her heart as it slammed against her breasts. Every instinct demanded that she cry out to Forrester for help, but she couldn't—not after what had just happened between them. At the moment she was even more terrified of him than of whatever it was that was happening to her.

She staggered back away from his outstretched hand and up against a tree, her fingers clawing at the front of her shirt. Her normally pale complexion was now totally devoid of colour, and there were spots swimming in front of her eyes.

Sam followed, muttering an offer of help, but Bernadette knocked his hand away with a choked cry.

Her huge, anguished eyes fixed on him in terror as her
legs gave way and she slid to the ground. If he attacked
her now, she would be at his mercy.

'No!' she gasped. 'No! Please! Leave ... me ...
alone!'

He swore softly and withdrew a pace, his body tense.
'It's an anxiety attack,' he told her curtly. 'It's all right,
Bernie. There's nothing physically wrong with you,
you're just afraid, that's all.'

Her next gasping breath cut short an hysterical laugh
that intensified the guilt already wrenching at him and
caused his hands to flex in impotent, self-directed anger.

'If you don't want me to touch you, I won't,' he
promised, holding her eyes as he sank down on his
haunches in front of her. 'But at least listen and do
what I tell you. All right?'

He didn't wait for her to agree. He started quietly
coaching her, and gradually she began to regain control
and her breathing became less tortured. She was still
gasping, afraid that any minute her tenuous control
would disappear again or else he'd make a sudden lunge
for her, but as the seconds dragged into minutes and
neither happened, she began to relax by slow degrees.

'Better?' Sam murmured, and she nodded, letting her
eyelids droop in exhausted relief. When she heard him
move, she tensed, but no strong, ruthless hands gripped
her and no dominating mouth resumed its diabolical
torment.

'Here,' he said, and she opened her eyes to look at
him. He was on one knee at her side, the whisky bottle
in his hand. 'Take a small drink. It'll steady your
nerves.'

The laugh that escaped her was wild, and she jerked
her head away as the bottle approached.

'Drink!' Sam ordered tersely, then took hold of her
chin and tipped the bottle to her mouth, nearly
drowning her with the fiery liquor.

Bernadette choked and sputtered, but eventually she
had to swallow. When he released her, the whisky that
had overflowed her mouth had saturated the front of
her shirt. She smelled like a moonshine still, and looked

like God knew what. She glared at him as she scooted
back against the tree, drawing her knees up to shield
her soaked, nearly transparent shirt front.

Forrester's mouth twitched as he observed her
indignant expression. 'Bit late for a show of modesty,
isn't it?' he drawled, then caught her wrist with a frown
when she tried to slap his face.

'Oh, no. I don't care to be struck, scratched, bitten,
kicked, or butted any more today, thank you.' He
released her with a warning look, then glanced down at
his left arm, where fresh blood stained the sleeve.

Bernadette's gaze followed his, her eyes widening.
'Did I hurt you?' she asked with quiet concern.

Forrester's head came around in surprise. 'You can't
be for real,' he murmured after a moment. 'Not ten
minutes ago you were ready to blow a hole in me!'

She shook her head firmly in denial. 'I wouldn't have.
You knew that. And anyway, you did provoke me.' She
held his eyes in accusation. 'You scared me half out of
my mind!'

Sam couldn't help thinking that if that was how she
reacted when she was scared, he hoped to hell he never
made her mad. He bent his head and studied the
ground until he had his amusement under control.

'Mmm. Well, I'll apologise if you will,' he offered as
he lifted his head and met her accusing eyes.

'*Me!* What have *I* got to apologise for?' Bernadette
demanded with righteous indignation.

He turned the right side of his face towards her.
'This, for one thing,' he drawled, running a finger down
the scratches on his cheek, 'And this.' He lifted his shirt
to reveal where she'd bitten him. 'And these.' Sitting on
the ground, he rolled up both trouser legs. There were a
couple of places where her heels had scraped the skin
from his shins, and Bernadette had no doubt he'd be
black and blue from the knees down by this time
tomorrow. 'Not to mention one clawed hand, a punch
in the jaw that didn't leave a mark, and this,' indicating
the spreading bloodstain on his left sleeve.

'Well?' His eyebrows rose expectantly, and he waited.

Bernadette knew she was blushing furiously. 'I can't

believe I did all that,' she muttered, then bit her lip in chagrin. 'Of course I apologise. But you *did* ask for it, you know,' she couldn't help adding defensively.

Forrester released a heavy sigh. 'I know. Believe me, I know. If it's any consolation, you can be damned sure I'll never make such a bloody fool of myself again.' His mouth thinned in self-disgust as he abruptly got to his feet and bent to push down his trouser legs.

Bernadette was a little bewildered. She'd be the first to agree that he'd behaved like a jackass, but after all, it hadn't been entirely his fault. It was humiliating to admit it, even to herself, but she had been more than just receptive; had, in fact, shamelessly invited what had happened.

'It won't happen again,' Sam repeated grimly as he straightened and looked down at her from what seemed a great height. 'You have my word on that, Sister.'

Sister? *Sister!* Oh, no! She cringed inside. Of course he was assuming all the blame! She might have forgotten, but obviously *he* hadn't.

'Why don't we just forget the whole thing,' Bernadette suggested hastily, her voice husky from nerves and guilt. 'I mean ... I'm willing to forgive and forget, if you are.'

Sam's mouth twisted with what could have been either mockery or bitterness. 'Of course, you would be. Forgiveness *is* your line, isn't it? All right, then.' He offered his hand, and after a second's hesitation, Bernadette took it.

'Friends?'

She nodded. 'Friends.' Suddenly much too aware of his firm, warm grip, she withdrew her hand and came off the ground to stand in front of him. 'I'd better rebandage your arm.'

Forrester nodded, and then his mouth quirked and a twinkle came into his eyes. Bernadette wondered at the sudden change of mood, until she realised that he was looking down at the front of her shirt. She quickly turned her back, shooting him an irritated glance over her shoulder.

'I think before we get around to my arm, I'd better

give you this,' he remarked drily as he went to his pack.
When he returned he was carrying a neatly folded,
brand new shirt. He turned her by a shoulder and
pushed it into her hand.

'I got it at Aggie's. I hope it's the right size.'

'Thank you,' Bernadette murmured, her voice
subdued.

She was touched that he'd thought to buy it for her.
It was a kind gesture, the act of a considerate man, she
reflected as she ducked behind some bushes to change.
How on earth was she supposed to reconcile *that* man
with the one she'd confronted just minutes ago?

He was such a complex, confusing character; just
when she thought she'd figured him out, he went and
did something totally unexpected. Would she ever fit all
the puzzle pieces together? And more important, was
she sure she wanted to?

CHAPTER TEN

BERNADETTE slept like the dead that night, unaware that she was watched over through most of it by a silent, brooding sentinel. The morning's first hazy light disclosed a dozen scattered cigarette butts and a handful of cheroot stubs, as well as two prone forms. The larger of them had been asleep for less than an hour.

It was some time later when a single shaft of sunlight penetrated the foliage overhead and slanted across Bernadette's face. Accustomed to being rousted out at the crack of dawn, she was first surprised, and then alarmed at the lateness of the hour. She wriggled out of her sleeping bag, then hurried to Sam's side to reassure herself that he'd only overslept.

His soft snores alerted her that this was the case before she even reached him. Bernadette sat back on her heels, her gaze softening as she looked down at him. He wouldn't like it if he woke and caught her watching him, she knew. She could imagine the way his thick, almost straight eyebrows would draw together over his nose and his eyes would narrow in irritation. He'd resent being caught with his guard down, vulnerable.

She smiled at the thought. Right now, his harsh features smoothed and relaxed, he did seem much softer, more approachable. He was lying on his back, one arm flung out to the side and the other resting across his chest. His head was turned towards her, giving her the opportunity to study that rugged face at her leisure.

It was a good face—strong and confident, with no sign of weakness in it. His nose was a little on the large side, with a bump in the middle. It had probably been broken at some time, possibly in a barroom fight, she thought in amusement. The well-defined fullness of his relaxed mouth surprised her a little. She couldn't resist the temptation to lay her fingers on his lips, to see if they were really as soft as they looked in repose.

After only the briefest contact she snatched her hand away. It was trembling. Her breath caught and she closed her eyes, stunned by the knowledge that had ripped through her like a lightning bolt. Oh dear, how could she have let it happen? How *could* she? To be so stupid, so masochistic, as to fall in love with *him*!

Her first, instinctive reaction was anger—at herself. There was absolutely no excuse for this pathetic situation. Of all the men to have fallen for——! He'd bullied her, patronised her, mocked her, ignored her, laughed at her, and threatened her with rape; not to mention risking her life by dragging her with him through this godforsaken jungle. She could count the times he'd shown her kindness or consideration on the fingers of one hand. The closest he'd ever come to paying her a compliment was to tell her she was 'the damnedest woman', and he refused to even use her correct name most of the time—it was either the butchered 'Bernie', or 'Sister', which he usually made sound like an insult instead of a term of respect. His views on women and marriage she didn't even want to think about, but unfortunately she couldn't keep from it.

Oh, damn, damn, *damn*!

To give herself something to do, and hopefully work off some of the anger, she started scrounging for firewood. The aroma of coffee finally roused Sam from his slumber. He disappeared into the bushes briefly, then came to the fire, sinking down on his haunches to silently accept the tin cup Bernadette held out.

'Powdered eggs?' she offered, and he nodded, still mute and apparently not feeling sociable. Bernadette accepted his withdrawn mood with a measure of relief. She could use some time to bludgeon her emotions into obedience, if not control.

'How's your arm?' she finally asked when the silence could be borne no longer.

Forrester turned a blank face to her. 'My arm? Oh ... my arm.' He flexed it, then shrugged. 'Fine. How are you feeling this morning?'

'Okay,' Bernadette lied with a smile that felt stiff.

He was frowning, his shrewd eyes scrutinising every feature of her wan face. 'Sure? Your system took quite a few shocks yesterday. It would be understandable if you felt a little off.'

'I said I was all right!' she repeated shortly as she turned away to start cleaning up. She didn't need reminding how many 'shocks' her system had taken in the last twenty-four hours, and she for damned sure didn't want to talk about it.

'You're still angry with me,' he said on a sigh.

'No, I'm not! Will you just——' Bernadette paused to take a deep, cleansing breath. 'I'm not angry,' she said more calmly. 'And if I was, it wouldn't be with you.'

Forrester was silent for several seconds. When he spoke, his deep voice was soft, and more sincere than she'd ever heard it.

'I hope you're not angry with yourself. You have no reason to be—everything that happened was my fault, and mine alone. If you need to blame someone, blame me.'

Bernadette closed her eyes tight. Oh Lord, why didn't he just shut up! He was only making it worse, increasing her agitation. When his hand came to rest on her shoulder she jerked away, unable to tolerate his touch.

'Please don't do that,' she said, her voice strained. 'And who says I'm blaming anybody? I just don't want to talk about it, all right? We said we'd forget it ever happened.'

'We also said we'd be friends,' Sam responded harshly. 'But how are we supposed to manage that when you can't even stand to look at me—Bernie, for God's sake, don't you realise——' He, too, took time for a deep, steadying breath. 'You can't possibly feel any worse this morning than I do,' he claimed wearily.

'Don't bet on it,' Bernadette muttered. 'I'll have everything packed away and ready to go in just a few minutes.'

She saw his features tense out of the corner of her eye as she rose, but he didn't comment. He busied himself rearranging the contents of his pack, but when

Bernadette had extinguished the fire and was tugging
hers on, he rose and came towards her, the small
revolver in his hand.

'Yes,' he said, forestalling her refusal to wear it. He
collected the gunbelt from the ground and deftly
buckled it around her hips. 'You'll take it, and you'll
wear it, and if the need arises, you'll use it,' he told her
in a flat, emotionless voice. He looked up, straight into
her eyes. 'Against anything or anyone that makes you
feel threatened. Including me.'

Bernadette shook her head, her eyes wounded. Surely
he didn't believe she could actually use a gun on him?
Didn't he realise that yesterday she'd only been reacting
instinctively, out of fear and anger?

'I—No,' she whispered, appalled by the very thought
of wearing the hateful thing again.

'Yes!' He removed the pistol from its holster, then
curled her cold, trembling fingers around it. His eyes
were as hard as his voice. 'It's got a hair trigger. I
should have told you that before.' Bernadette felt a
convulsive shudder go through her, but he ignored the
reaction and continued in the same flat, impersonal
tone. 'To cock it, you pull back on the hammer, like
this.' He moved her thumb to demonstrate. 'It'll fire
without being cocked, but it requires a lot more
pressure—you'd probably need both hands. This is half
cock,' as the hammer clicked once, 'and this full cock.
At full cock, you only need to breathe hard on the
trigger mechanism to fire it.'

He placed his finger over hers and lifted her arm,
pointing the gun into the branches overhead, then
applied the slightest degree of pressure. Bernadette
started violently when the pistol discharged in her hand,
but once again he ignored her response.

'It doesn't have much of a kick, and it's a fairly
accurate piece,' he said as he removed the weapon from
her numbed grasp and tucked it back in the holster. 'At
close range, one shot at the head or upper chest could
kill a man. Or a woman,' he added, his mouth grim.
Bernadette felt the blood drain from her face as she
remembered holding the cold metal against her temple.

Something of her horror must have shown, because
Forrester's gaze suddenly softened. He reached out to
test the buckle of the gunbelt, and then the straps of her
pack, and when he spoke again his voice held more
warmth.

'It was a mistake not to have shown you how to use
it at the very beginning,' he murmured. 'But damned if
I thought you'd ever take it out of the holster.' He
looked into her eyes, his expression guarded. 'Feel more
secure, now? Safer?'

Bernadette swallowed and shook her head. 'No. It
terrifies me. I'll never touch it again.'

'I hope you never feel the need to. But if you do——'

'What kind of person do you think I am?' she
interrupted shrilly. 'What do you think I've turned into
in the last few days, that I could calmly aim a gun at
someone and pull the trigger?'

She was staring at him in shock and dismay, hurt
that he could believe her capable of such a thing.

'Whatever you've turned into in the last few days, the
credit or blame lies at my door,' Sam replied curtly.
'You didn't ask for anything that's happened to you.
Your only concern was to get a bunch of children and
an old lady safely home. I told you in the beginning
that I'd get us both out of this mess alive and
unharmed. We both know what a miserable job I've
done of keeping you unharmed, but by God I *will* get
you out, Sister! And when I have, you can go to your
priest and confess whatever sins you think you may
have committed. But as God is my witness, it'll be a
long time before I'll be able to look at myself in the
mirror without feeling sick to my stomach!'

He turned away suddenly, leaving her to stare at his
broad back in astonishment. She wanted to go to him,
to put her arms around him and tell him the truth, to
ease the guilt she could sense was tormenting him. She
could never be sure what stopped her, unless it was a
deep-seated instinct for self-preservation. In order to
give him comfort, she would have had to sacrifice the
protection her role provided, and risk the consequences.
It caused her great pain to acknowledge that she

couldn't do that; especially not now, not after this morning's shattering revelation.

By noon Bernadette was firmly convinced that God Almighty was punishing her in the worst way possible for having had the audacity to impersonate a nun: He had caused her to lose her heart to the Devil, himself, and was probably sitting back on His Heavenly throne with a smile of righteous satisfaction as He observed her torment. Every step carried them closer to their destination, to the time when they would part company, go their separate ways. She was in agony at the prospect, but could see no way to avoid the inevitable. Nothing had changed; certainly not Forrester, anyway. One week in her company was hardly likely to have altered his outlook on life or his basic personality.

When they stopped for a cold lunch, Bernadette shed her pack to trudge listlessly into the bushes. This time it wasn't nature's call that drew her from his side, but a desperate need to be alone, to try and gain some control over her turbulent emotions. She didn't notice the sharp look Sam gave her as she passed him, glassy-eyed and moving like a robot, nor did she hear his soft, concerned query.

She halted in a small, sunlight-dappled clearing some yards away, unaware of anything but her own misery. After a brief struggle against the urge to break down and cry, she gave in. Maybe what she needed was to just let go and get it over with, to indulge in a single, cathartic orgy of weeping. She fell to her knees, pressing her clasped hands to her mouth in an attempt to stifle her sobs, so he wouldn't hear.

When Sam came up behind her, he naturally mistook her position to be one of prayer, and started to back away. Then he saw the way her shoulders jerked and heard her muffled sobs. He went rigidly still, his mouth twisting in a spasm of remorse and his hands clenching at his sides. And then he quietly slipped away, back the way he had come, leaving her alone with her pain.

When Bernadette returned, no mention was made of how long she'd been gone; in fact, not a word was spoken by either of them. She shouldered her way into her pack and when he started off, she followed, pale and subdued but much more at peace with herself and the situation.

The same could not be said of Forrester. Seeing her crying her heart out on her knees had hit him like a kick in the stomach. What the hell kind of man was he, anyway? Where did he get off treating her so callously, with such an insulting lack of simple human decency? Because she'd always been so spunky, so outspoken, he'd allowed himself to forget that she was a nun—a *nun*, for God's sake! Innocent, at least until she'd had the miserable luck to fall in with him. He had to be the lowest form of low-life there was!

He remembered her reaction when he would have left the lion cub behind, the way she'd calmly told him that she wouldn't have it on her conscience; that she felt responsible for the mother's death and would *not* be responsible for the cub's, as well. How many so-called women would have shown that much compassion, that much respect for life?

And yet she also possessed such surprising strength and courage. He'd seen both, repeatedly, and never failed to be impressed. She was the only woman he'd ever met—and to be honest, there'd been damn few men—who'd refused to back down under his bullying and his surly temper. What's more, she had a temper of her own, and she wasn't afraid to show it.

He sighed heavily as he shrugged to ease the strain between his shoulders. What was she thinking as she walked along behind him? Was she hating him? No, he doubted it was in her to hate, really hate. He wished she could. If just once he saw hate or loathing in her eyes, maybe he'd find it easier to live with this unaccustomed guilt.

They made a morosely silent twosome as they trekked on through the afternoon, each absorbed in private thoughts. Bernadette was just beginning to emerge from her self-involvement when without warning Forrester spun around and lunged for her. Her eyes flew wide as he clamped a hand over her mouth and dragged her into a group of tall, fernlike plants. She twisted her head to question him with an alarmed look. His palm pressed against her lips in warning, and then he placed his mouth to her ear and released her.

'Men up ahead,' he breathed. 'Coming this way. Give me your gun.'

She did so without hesitation, then looked at him fearfully. He shook his head with a frown which she supposed was meant to be reassuring as he tucked her pistol into the back of his belt.

'Don't be afraid,' he whispered, and then he astounded her by laying his hand along her cheek and dropping a gentle kiss on her forehead. 'And stay right here!'

Before she could even nod, he was gone, moving so quickly and quietly that it was impossible to follow his passage through the undergrowth. Deprived of the opportunity for positive action, Bernadette clasped her hands in front of her and started praying.

Oh, God, please keep him safe ... please! I can understand Your being annoyed with me, but he hasn't done anything to be punished for, not really. It's just his way to be arrogant and bossy, but underneath all that he's a good man, God, You know he is. Oh, please don't let him be hurt! If You'll keep him safe, I'll—I'll——

She was trying frantically to think of something to bargain with, when a loud shout made her nearly jump out of her shoes. She tensed for the gunfire she knew would follow, her heart racing and her mouth dry. Instead of a shot, she heard Sam's bellowed 'Bernie!', and almost collapsed in hysterical relief.

'It's all right—they're friends. Come on out.'

Somehow she managed to go to him on legs that felt like overcooked spaghetti, and when she reached his side he hooked an arm around her waist and smiled down at her.

'They're Tzongari's men,' he explained as she glanced nervously at the semi-circle of grinning faces before them. 'He's camped a couple of kilometres from here.' He paused for effect, then added with a wicked grin: 'And his camp has a cook, tents, and plenty of fresh water. Sound good?'

'Sounds like Heaven,' Bernadette answered fervently.

He released her to remove the pistol from his belt and handed it over. 'Better take this back,' he advised, watching her face.

Bernadette nodded as she accepted the gun and slipped it into its holster. 'Thanks,' she murmured drily. 'I feel naked without it.'

The quick smile that lit Sam's eyes was compensation enough for all she'd been through, and her feet seemed to float over the earth as they fell in behind the patrol of Prince Tzongari's troops.

Three hours later Bernadette was lounging in a canvas folding chair, sipping at a mug of steaming fresh-ground coffee while Forrester conferred with the Prince in his tent. She and her clothing were clean, she'd been fed a sumptuous meal, and later she would retire to the tent that had been assigned her. She placed her mug on the table in front of her and smiled at Claude Dorleac, seated across it.

'You could have knocked me over with a feather when we came into camp and I saw you standing there next to the Prince.'

He grinned back at her. 'I know. You looked like you couldn't decide whether to kiss me or hit me over the head with something. Had a trying week, have you, Soeur Bernadette?'

She grimaced and lowered her eyes. 'You could say that.'

'But not nearly so trying as poor Sam, n'est-ce pas? From the looks of him, he must have tangled with a pride of lions, at the very least. Or perhaps just one angry she-cat,' he murmured as he lifted his own mug and hid a grin behind it.

'Oh sure, laugh,' Bernadette muttered. Then she saw the situation from his point of view, and an involuntary smile tugged at her mouth. 'He asked for every one of those scratches.'

One of Claude's fair brows lifted. 'And more, I would expect. They look fresh, though. Your ... mm, disguise, seems to have served you well for the first several days, at least.'

'When I could remember to make use of it,'
Bernadette agreed drily. 'Which reminds me, I intended
to thank you for slipping the word to the Prince before
we got here.'

Claude shrugged. 'If a man hadn't returned ahead of
you to tell him Sam was coming in, I wouldn't have had
the chance. He thought it was all a marvellous joke,' he
added with another grin. 'Though I suspect he'll just as
soon not be around when Sam learns the truth.'

'That makes two of us,' Bernadette said with feeling.

'And well you might worry,' Claude taunted. 'He's
liable to pay you back for those scratches, and then go
you one better.'

Bernadette flashed him a resentful look. 'Need I
remind you, *Monsieur*, that you're the one who got me
into this mess? If you hadn't deliberately arranged for
him to overhear us saying goodbye——'

'He would have had your clothes off before I'd even
retracted my landing gear,' Claude interrupted, and her
cheeks flamed as she cast a frantic look around them.

'Will you keep your voice down! And for God's sake,
do you have to be so crude!' she hissed.

His eyes glittered with mischief as he sipped at his
coffee. 'I was only speaking the truth. He wanted you
badly, Bernadette. I saw it, and so did your Mrs
Althoff.' He ignored her shocked gasp and went on
calmly. 'And whatever has happened between you since
then, it hasn't diminished his desire. He looks at you
like a starving man would look at a banquet table, and
can hardly bear to have you out of his sight. If it didn't
seem so out of character, I'd say he's behaving exactly
like a man in love,' he reflected in amusement.

'Don't be ridiculous!' Bernadette snapped irritably.
'Out of character, is right! That man thinks women
were put on this earth for one thing, and one thing
only, and damned if I'll be one of his ships that pass in
the night! I have a little more respect for myself than
that, Claude!'

'But of course you do, *chérie*, and so do I,' he
soothed, reaching over to place a hand over hers.
'Which was why I risked my very life by tricking him as

I did. Surely you cannot be resentful because I wished to provide you with some sort of protection?'

'No, of course not,' Bernadette admitted on a sigh. 'I just wish to God this farce was over, that's all. You can't imagine what a strain it's been. Lord, and to think I once actually considered entering a convent! I wouldn't have lasted a week!'

'Three days, at the most,' he agreed, and they both laughed.

'Care to share the joke?'

Bernadette looked up in surprise, and found Forrester and Prince Tzongari standing beside the table. The Prince's eyes held an amused gleam, but Sam's face wore a scowl which sobered her instantly.

'It was nothing,' Claude answered carelessly. 'A small . . .' he darted a quick glance at Bernadette and his mouth twitched, 'religious joke, you might say. The humour would be lost on a sinner such as yourself.'

Forrester's frown deepened and his nostrils pinched. Bernadette glanced away from the cold anger in his eyes and happened to meet the stoic stare of Prince Tzongari. She nearly fell out of her chair when he deliberately lowered one eyelid in a sly wink.

And then he was ordering more chairs to be brought, and a cassette player so that he and his guests could enjoy some music. Bernadette sat as still as a statue, afraid to do or say anything which might bring this extraordinary scene to a climax. Claude was playing the suave Frenchman to the hilt, their host had apparently decided to turn on his considerable charm, as well, and between them—directly across the table from Bernadette—Forrester sat stonily silent, growing more grim by the second.

She discovered that the Prince wasn't at all the aloof, slightly cold man she'd taken him to be on his visits to the school. Tall and muscular, he was obviously well-educated, and possessed an easygoing charm that soon had her relaxing despite herself. He insisted that she call him James, or Tzongari, if she preferred; one was his English name, the other his African name, and he was

comfortable with either. But he asked that she refrain
from using the royal title.

'You see,' he explained with a grin, 'in this part of
Africa, almost everyone and his cousin George can lay
claim to at least one ancestor who was a king. Isn't that
right, Sam?'

Forrester snorted into his glass before he drained it.
He'd been helping himself to liberal amounts of
Tzongari/James's imported cognac, to the detriment of
his already sullen temper.

'And if the rest of the men hereabouts are as randy as
you, they probably all share the *same* ancestor,' he
jeered.

Bernadette blanched in fear for him, but their host
didn't seem at all put out. He merely clucked his tongue
and waggled a finger under Forrester's nose.

'And aren't you a fine one to be giving *me* lectures
about women,' he scoffed. 'Sam Forrester, whose
reputation as a womaniser rivals his reputation as a
soldier.'

'You don't see me cuddled up with half-a-dozen
wives, do you?' Forrester growled in reply. 'There
ought to be a law.'

'Ah, but there is,' his friend assured him. 'It says that
a man may have as many wives as he can support, and
fortunately for me, I can support quite a few.'

'It's disgusting,' Forrester declared as he poured
himself another brandy.

'Marriage?' Claude asked with a grin in Bernadette's
direction. She frowned at him, but he refused to take
the hint as he sat back to enjoy the rest of the show.

'No, not marriage!' Forrester muttered irritably.
'There's nothing wrong with marriage, in itself, if a man
and woman are suited. But it should be *a* man and *a*
woman, you bloody heathen! One of each, and that's all!'

The Prince nodded soberly. 'Ah, now I understand.
You are an advocate of monogamy. Well then, tell me
this, my friend . . .' he suddenly leaned forward, shoving
his face close to Forrester's with a wicked grin, 'if you
are so sold on marriage, why is it that you're still a
bachelor at the ripe old age of . . .'

'Forty-four,' Bernadette supplied, and earned a fierce glare for her trouble.

Claude snorted rudely before Forrester could reply. 'What woman in her right mind would have him?'

'Good point,' Tzongari remarked with a gleaming smile. 'He isn't exactly the catch of the year, is he?'

'Thanks,' Forrester muttered, sending a disgusted look around the table and then downing another ounce of cognac.

'He smokes too much,' Bernadette chimed in helpfully. 'And swears like a drunken sailor. And he isn't exactly overflowing with the milk of human kindness, either, not to mention his rotten temper.'

'By all means, let's not mention my temper,' Forrester growled. 'God knows I've got the shortest fuse on the face of the planet. I've even been known to go completely berserk from time to time, with no provocation whatsoever.'

Bernadette cleared her throat and dropped her eyes. 'Yes, well, ... I suppose there are people with worse tempers,' she mumbled under her breath.

'But overall,' Claude considered thoughtfully, 'he does seem to have more than his share of faults, n'est-ce pas? Hardly a prize catch, would you think, Soeur Bernadette?'

She gave his leg a savage kick under the table, but before she could reply Forrester apparently decided he'd had enough. His glass slammed down and he unfolded himself from his chair to loom over them all.

'I'm so glad that's settled,' he muttered with heavy sarcasm. 'The verdict's in—I'm a miserable wretch who doesn't deserve to breathe the same air as the rest of humanity. All agreed? Right, then.'

He came around to yank Bernadette's chair back from the table, nearly dumping her on the ground in the process.

'I want to dance,' he growled. 'On your feet, Sister, or I'll probably tear you limb from limb in a manic rage.'

She tried and failed to keep from smiling as he dragged her between two tents. Just as he pulled her

close and his arms slipped around her, someone
changed the tape cassette and a soft, decidedly romantic
instrumental began to play. Bernadette's arms lifted to
his neck, but he pulled them away and put them around
his waist, instead.

'And whose benefit is this performance for?' she
asked drily, but she didn't attempt to move out of his
embrace.

'Mine. Feeling better?'

'Much.' She let her cheek rest against his shoulder
and listened to the slow, regular thud of his heart. 'How
about you?'

'Oh, I'm in great shape, considering I've just had the
hide stripped off me by three razor sharp tongues,' he
drawled. He waited a moment, then murmured in a too-
casual voice: 'I have a proposition for you.'

Bernadette's eyes darted upward, but she didn't lift
her head. 'I'm listening.'

'What would you say to the idea of starting over,
from scratch? If we really work at it, we just *might* end
up as friends. Stranger things have happened.'

Bernadette closed her eyes against a swell of
bittersweet emotion so intense it was painful. Why not?
Why not take whatever she could share with him, grab
with both hands, while she could?

'Sounds good to me,' she said huskily.

'Does it? Because I'm serious,' he murmured intently.
'I'd like us to keep in touch. Who knows, maybe some
day I'll even drop by your school for a visit.'

Oh, if only he would! She'd know then that he felt
something for her, something more than just sexual
attraction. And would he be in for the surprise of his life!

'I'd like that,' she told him, smiling against his chest.
'If you let me know you're coming, I'll bake you a
pecan pie.'

Sam bent his head so that his mouth hovered over
her ear. 'It's a deal. You don't wear one of those
getups, do you?' he demanded suddenly, as if the
thought had just occurred to him.

'You mean a habit?' Bernadette asked with a grin.
'No, I don't wear a habit.'

'Good. I think I'd have trouble dealing with that. Besides, I don't care if you are a nun, it would be a sin to hide a figure like yours in one of those shapeless sacks.'

'Colonel!' Bernadette said in mild reproach.

'Sam,' he corrected softly.

'Sam,' she whispered.

They shuffled around in slow circles for a while, not speaking, and Bernadette thought she'd never felt closer to another human being in her life.

When the tape finally came to an end he released her, slowly and reluctantly, then took her hand to lead her back to the table. The two men rose at their approach, wearing identical, idiotic grins. In their absence, Claude had switched places. Not too subtle, Bernadette thought in amusement as Forrester seated her and then took the vacant chair on her left. It seemed to be several inches closer than when Claude had occupied it. A fresh mug of coffee was placed before her, but before she could pick it up Sam replaced it with a small glass of cognac.

'You're entitled,' he said in answer to her questioning look.

'Careful, Sam,' Claude warned. 'Someone might imagine that you're trying to get her drunk.'

'Not bloody likely,' Forrester growled as he leaned back and took out a cheroot. 'She could drink all three of us under the table.' He drew deeply on the cigar, then added with a trace of admiration, 'She's also got a lulu of a left hook.'

Bernadette sipped daintily at her brandy and let their conversation flow around her, and basked in the glow of the lazy smiles Sam gave her now and then as he lounged in his chair. They might have been an old married couple, enjoying an after-dinner drink with two friends on the patio. Only if they had been, the friends would eventually leave and they'd go inside . . . to bed . . . together. Her soft sigh was wistful as she stared down into her empty glass. Goodness, when had she finished off the brandy in it?

Hearing the sigh, Forrester leaned towards her with a tender, questioning smile that made her heart capsize.

'Tired?' he murmured.

'Just a bit,' Bernadette admitted breathlessly.

'And no wonder,' Claude remarked from across the table. 'This past week must have been quite an ordeal for you, in more ways than one.'

Bernadette smiled, pointedly ignoring the rather heavy innuendo. 'It's certainly been an experience,' she replied lightly.

The gleam in Claude's eye warned her he wasn't finished. 'Did I mention that I'm flying out in the morning? I would be more than happy to take you directly to Bulawayo. I could have you there in time for supper.'

Bernadette felt Sam's eyes on her. She turned her head and lifted her delicate brows, letting him know the decision was his to make.

'Thanks, Claude,' he said, holding her eyes, 'but once I begin a job, I like to finish it.' His mouth tilted upward at one corner. 'Besides, we're a team. Right, Sister?'

'Right,' Bernadette agreed softly.

When a few minutes later she caught herself stifling a yawn, she decided it was time to turn in. She wavered between panic and elation when Sam rose with her and echoed her good nights, and after a brief struggle, elation won hands down.

He gripped her arm in a light clasp to guide her through the darkened camp, and waited until they were well away from the table before he spoke.

'I may have forgotten to mention—we're sharing a tent.'

'Oh?' Surprise made her voice crack.

'Mmm. You don't mind, do you?'

Did she? Of course she didn't; that was the trouble. 'Should I mind?' she asked in a subdued murmur.

'I don't see why. We've spent the last five nights sleeping together, figuratively speaking, of course. The only difference tonight is that we'll have walls surrounding us and a roof over our heads.'

Which was perfectly true, Bernadette told herself sensibly. She'd do well to emulate his mature attitude;

he sounded apathetic to the point of boredom. She frowned suspiciously as they reached the tent. Bored? By the prospect of sharing the seclusion of a tent with her? Not very likely!

He let her precede him inside, and she groped around in the dark for her sleeping bag. When she found it, she muttered under her breath in irritation.

'Not again!'

'What is it?' came the disinterested query from behind her.

Bernadette peered up at him from her knees, trying in vain to make out his features.

'Somebody's zipped our bags together again. Help me separate them, will you? I can't see a thing in the dark.'

She felt him come down beside her, and tensed involuntarily at his nearness.

'Why bother?' he said lazily.

'Wh-why *bother*?' she echoed. Then, her voice growing sharp, 'What do you mean, why bother?'

His shoulder nudged hers as he shrugged. 'With no light, we could be an hour sorting it all out.'

'Well you could go get a flashlight or something, couldn't you!'

He didn't answer immediately. He edged away, and Bernadette squinted as she tried to follow his movements.

'I could,' he drawled after a while, then yawned hugely. 'But I'm not going to. I'm too tired to go tramping from tent to tent begging a torch. Besides, you're making a mountain out of a molehill.'

His attitude temporarily put Bernadette at a loss for words. He sounded totally indifferent ... *bored*, she thought again. She felt insulted. How *dare* he be bored!

'What are you doing?' she demanded as she made out the hunched shape of his shoulders.

'Taking off my boots. Ahh, that feels good.'

Bernadette's lips clamped together. All right, damn him, if he could be indifferent, so could she! She nearly broke her shoelaces yanking them loose, then set her shoes to one side and removed her gunbelt. It went on top of the shoes. She felt rather than saw him move closer.

'We'll sleep on top of the bags, all right?'

It wasn't a question, despite the way he'd phrased it. The arrogant swine was ordering her around *again*!

'Fine,' Bernadette said between stiff lips.

This time she remembered her 'prayers'. By the time she'd finished heaping mental abuse on his head, Sam was stretched out comfortably behind her. She joined him, keeping a good foot of space between them, her body tense and still. She almost wished he would make a move, give her an excuse to light into him. By God, he'd think twice before he treated her like a piece of furniture again!

'All done?' His voice was a soft rasp in the dark.

'Yes,' Bernadette muttered.

'Good.' He suddenly rolled, his arms coming out to gather her to him, one long leg hooking over hers so naturally that at first she didn't react. Then she stiffened, trying to pull away as the intimacy of his embrace brought an unwanted warmth to her blood.

'Sam! Don't! Let go!'

'No,' he refused calmly, dragging her closer. 'I don't want to let you go, and I'm not going to. Not for tonight, anyway. I didn't go to all the trouble of arranging to share a tent with you, then sneaking in here to fix our sleeping bags——'

'*You!*' Bernadette gasped, her muscles going lax in surprise.

'That's right.' He pulled back a little, his eyes glinting like silver coins as they searched the barely discernible features of her face. 'I want to spend one night, one whole night, with you in my arms,' he said quietly. 'Not to make love to you—oh, I want that, I'd be lying if I said I don't—but I'll settle for just holding you, feeling you next to me. And this is the last chance I'll have. I'm sending you with Claude in the morning.'

CHAPTER ELEVEN

'Why?' Bernadette asked when she could trust her voice not to betray her heartache.

'Because I have to,' Sam said roughly. 'Because if I don't——' He broke off abruptly, and in the electric silence which followed Bernadette felt every nerve in her body quiver with expectancy. *Please*, her heart cried out to him; *oh, please! I love you!*

She felt him forcing himself to relax, literally willing himself back under control. One of his hands lifted to her face, his fingers exploring softly, almost reverently, tracing every feature as if he was trying to imprint the shape and texture of her on his memory for all time.

'You look . . . feel, so fragile,' he murmured in a hushed voice. 'I keep thinking of everything you've been through in the last week, and I marvel at your strength. You fill me with wonder. You're everything woman was meant to be, and more . . . so much more. A man could lose himself in you, ransom his soul to be near you, forget to eat or sleep or breathe, until he existed solely for the hope of one of your smiles, the touch of your hand. It isn't fair. There's no justice in it—for the Almighty to have put everything a man could ever want, all he could dream of, in one woman, and then place her beyond his reach.'

Bernadette lay in overwhelmed silence under the gentle caress of his hand. What was he saying? What was he telling her? His beautiful, haunting words had been spoken in an almost desolate voice. He sounded, . . . he sounded like he was grieving!

She knew when he frowned, could see his deep forehead crease in her mind's eye, the way his shaggy black brows drew together.

'I've known a lot of women in my life,' he told her quietly. 'None of them gave me much reason to think well of the female of the species. Oh, once or twice one came along who made me believe she was different—

special. But then I'd catch her in a lie, discover she'd been deliberately deceiving me. The hell of it was, not a one seemed to mind being found out all that much. They took the attitude that I shouldn't have expected anything different. I'd come to the conclusion that women just didn't have it in them to be honest, that there was some chromosome missing or something that caused them all to be pathological liars and cheats. And then I met you,' he murmured, and Bernadette felt a cold, clammy dread clutch at her stomach.

'That first night, in your hotel room, I thought you were just like all the rest—stringing me along, playing Little Miss Innocent, pandering to a woman's idea of what the male ego requires.' His voice became drily amused as he added, 'I soon discovered how wrong I was, and believe me, I've never been more pleasantly surprised in my life. You were different. You were unique.' He sighed, his thumb slowly stroking her cheek.

'I was really looking forward to seeing you that next morning. I'd made up my mind to win you over, by fair means or foul, but I could tell you were still mad at me for making a pass, so I decided to play it cool for a while. Then, when I figured you'd had time to get over your miff and tried to be friendly, you blocked my every move, always sniping at me, giving me the feeling you could see right through to my soul and didn't much like what you saw. I was annoyed, but at the same time you were the most intriguing woman I'd ever met. And of course I wanted you, even then.'

Bernadette felt her cheeks grow warm. So Claude had been right about that. Had he also been right about Mrs Althoff knowing? The thought alone was enough to make her burn with embarrassment. Oh Lord, would she even have a job left, after spending six days and nights alone with him? And yet, Mrs A had been surprisingly willing to leave her behind with this man who admitted to even then having had designs on her virtue.

Sam's voice interrupted her musings. 'Needless to say, it came as quite a shock to discover you were a nun,' he drawled. 'I felt a blithering idiot, an absolute *fool*, and I could have wrung your neck for letting me make such an ass of myself. That was the only time you failed to be completely honest with me. You lied by omission.'

Oh, if it was only that simple! And how could she tell him the truth, when he kept eulogising her, making her sound like a candidate for sainthood?

'Of course, looking back, I can understand how you never got around to telling me,' he went on, simultaneously excusing and damning her. 'I've treated you abominably, Bernie, and I'm more sorry than I can say.'

The humble note in his gravelly voice made her want to writhe with guilt. When he lowered his head to place soft, repentant kisses on her eyelids, tears of remorse spurted behind them.

'Forgive me, if you can?' he asked in a husky whisper.

Bernadette shook her head. 'There's nothing to forgive. Oh, Sam, if you only knew——'

'Shh, shh, I do know.' His lips touched hers briefly, featherlight and so tender she didn't think she could bear it. 'I do,' he repeated softly. 'I've awakened feelings in you, aroused needs, that no man has the right to arouse. You think I don't know, that I can't feel the way you respond to me?' His voice was unsteady, and so was the deep breath he took, his chest expanding against hers. 'When I can think straight, it just gives me one more reason to despise myself. The trouble is, when I'm with you I'm not usually thinking straight.'

'It isn't a sin for two people to want each other—care for each other,' Bernadette tried again. This wasn't going to be easy. She had to break it to him gently, hopefully without provoking his anger or offending his pride. 'You do care for me, don't you? It isn't *just* wanting?'

He fell on to his side, hauling her against him in a bone-crushing embrace. 'I care,' he muttered roughly. 'Dear God, *yes*, I care!' He'd shaved earlier, and his smooth cheek rubbed against hers in agitation. Bernadette's heart took flight and soared. He loved her! He must!

'But I shouldn't,' he added in a grim, angry voice. 'Not like I do. You're a *nun*, Bernie!'

Was he reminding her, or himself?

'But if I wasn't?' Bernadette asked huskily. 'What if I wasn't a nun, Sam? If I suddenly became just a plain, ordinary schoolteacher? Would you——?'

'*No!*' he said fiercely. 'Oh no, don't lay that on me, on top of everything else! I couldn't let you give up your vows, not for me. I couldn't live with that on my conscience, too.'

'But I wouldn't be——' she tried to explain, and he cut her off by pressing a hard palm over her mouth.

'No! Don't say it, don't even think it!' he muttered. He took his hand away and pressed her face into his neck, and once again she felt him enforcing control, grimly subduing emotion, until the tension left his body and his arms held her with gentle strength.

'Don't say anything,' he murmured into her hair. 'Just lie here with me, and let me pretend that you're mine. Just for tonight, Bernie for tonight be mine . . . all mine.'

For tonight and as many nights as you want me, she promised silently as she snuggled close and slipped her arms around him, His raging arousal didn't shock her; on the contrary, she felt a smug pride to know she could affect him so easily, without even trying. She smiled as she closed her eyes. All right, then, for tonight she would just lie in his arms. But it would be the last time she did, without making love with him; because she had no intention of leaving with Claude in the morning. Come hell or high water, tomorrow morning she would tell him the truth, and then just let him *try* to get rid of her!

It might have been minutes or hours later when a shout outside woke Bernadette. While she struggled to throw off the muffling blanket of sleep, the first shout was followed by several more. She realised that Sam was fully awake and alert beside her; still, but primed for sudden movement.

'What——?'

'Sh! Quiet!' Seconds after muttering the curt command he released her and sat up in a single, fluid motion. Bernadette pushed up on her elbows in time to see him slide his pistol from its holster. He paused before lifting the tent flap to glance back at her.

'Take your gun out and stay here,' he ordered. And then he was gone, slipping outside in his stocking feet.

Bernadette didn't waste time on fear or indecision. Some deep, purely instinctive knowledge warned her that if she wanted to have any kind of future at all—let alone one with him—it was imperative that she do as he said. First she tugged on her shoes and then buckled the gunbelt around her waist. If Forrester had been there to watch, he'd have been proud of her clean, economical movements; not a motion was wasted. She drew the gun and then knelt facing the tent flap with it clasped in calm, steady hands.

There was the sound of a gunshot outside, and still she remained calm. Sam was all right, somehow she knew that, and the knowledge allowed her to wait patiently for him to return.

Suddenly the tent flap was jerked aside and bright, artificial light spilled through, silhouetting the figure stooped over to enter. When Sam looked up, he was greeted by the sight of Bernadette on her knees, her pistol aimed at the centre of his forehead. He froze for an instant in surprise, then frowned and ducked inside.

'I hope you don't intend making a habit of that,' he muttered. 'It could cause a person to become a bit paranoid.'

Bernadette lowered the pistol and eased the hammer back down. His eyes narrowed when he detected the movement.

'Great,' he drawled. 'I've created the world's first terrorist nun.'

She wasn't amused. 'What was all the excitement about?'

'One of the guards spotted a man just outside the perimeter. Get your gear together, we may be leaving in a hurry.'

'In the middle of the night?' Bernadette protested.

'You'd rather stick around to see if it was one of the men from George's?' he countered drily.

'Give me five minutes.'

'You've got two.'

But as it turned out, she wasn't allowed even that much time. Just as she reached for the tab to unzip their sleeping bags there was a staccato burst of automatic weapon fire, and the next thing she knew she was lying face down with Sam spreadeagled on top of her.

'Damn,' he said irritably, then slid off her and bellycrawled his way to the front of the tent. 'Stay down!'

Bernadette lifted her head to call after him in alarm. 'Sam! Where are you——'

'Get your bloody head down, Bernie, and *keep* it down!'

This time he was back in seconds instead of minutes, Prince Tzongari right behind him. At almost the same moment they burst into the tent, a Land Rover screeched to a halt outside.

The Prince clamped a hand on Forrester's shoulder. 'Take the Rover and get her out of here fast. Eloise Althoff would have my head if anything happened to her.' He turned to smile warmly at Bernadette. '*Au revoir, Soeur Bernadette*. Give my love to my daughters, when you see them.'

Bernadette nodded dazedly. When she didn't move fast enough, Sam reached down to grab her arm and yank her to her feet.

'Beggin' your pardon, Sister, but could you please get your tail in gear,' he growled. 'Before it gets shot off!'

Bernadette half turned to reach for her pack, and he spun her back around, shoving her towards the front of the tent.

'Now, Bernie, *move*!'

It said a lot about their individual priorities that on the way out, he snatched up the rifle and she collected his boots.

'Doesn't take orders very well, does she?' Tzongari yelled as Forrester scooped her up and literally threw her into the passenger side of the Land Rover before running around to vault into the driver's seat.

'No way!' Sam roared back, then suddenly grinned. 'She never does what she's bloody well told, but at least she doesn't bore a man to death!'

Bernadette opened her mouth to fire off an indignant retort, then nearly severed her tongue when he released the clutch and the vehicle shot forward as if fired from a cannon.

He drives like a maniac, she thought as she gripped the sides of her seat to hold herself in it. Dear God, had the man never heard of brakes? If a stray bullet didn't kill her, his driving very well might.

She thought that once they were clear of the camp he would surely slow down, but such was not the case. They hurtled on through the night, at times barely keeping to the rutted, often all but invisible road. Bernadette locked her jaw to keep her teeth from being jarred loose. It was almost noon before they finally stopped, and from the way Sam swore, it wasn't because he'd decided to get out and stretch his legs.

'What is it? What's wrong?' Bernadette asked, not really caring. Whatever the problem was, she hoped it would take a while for him to fix. She could do with the rest.

'The bloody petrol's run out,' he muttered. Then, when she frowned at him: 'Gasoline. We're fresh out.'

'Oh. Well that's just great! Since you hustled us out of camp without even bringing food or the first-aid kit, that sort of leaves us up the proverbial creek, doesn't it?'

He turned towards her, resting his forearms on the steering wheel. 'My, my, testy when we haven't had our full eight hours, aren't we?' he drawled. 'As it happens, we're hardly more than half a day's walk from the Lubumbashi airport.'

'We are?' Bernadette was both relieved and depressed by the news.

'We are,' Sam confirmed tersely, then swung around and slid to the ground. 'But we won't get there by sitting on our backsides talking about it.'

They'd been walking for about two hours when they

happened upon one of the loveliest scenes Bernadette had ever beheld. A small waterfall cascaded about thrity feet down a sheer rock wall and ended in a shallow pool at the bottom. From there, a wide stream—or maybe it would be considered a narrow river—meandered away towards the south. When she exclaimed in delight, Sam smiled benignly and said they might as well stop for a while. She felt like hugging him, but couldn't quite work up the nerve. Since they'd set out on foot he'd been withdrawn, silent, and she suspected he was regretting the things he'd said in the tent the night before.

Tough luck if he was, she decided as she sat down on the stream bank and removed her shoes and socks to wiggle her toes in the cool water. She was just thinking that when they arrived at the airport would be the best time to spring the truth on him, when she saw the snake.

She scrabbled backward as fast as she could, but it wasn't quite fast enough. The small green serpent lashed out at her foot, and a white hot pain seared her ankle as its fangs sank in. Bernadette stared down at the bite marks in stunned surprise as the snake slithered away. She started to jump up and run to Sam, then thought better of it.

Don't get excited, she told herself firmly. *Don't panic or move around unnecessarily; you'll just spread whatever he put in there that much faster.*

She got slowly to her feet and made herself walk—not run—to where Forrester was stretched out on his back, studiouly contemplating the foliage overhead.

'Sam?' she said softly.'

'Mmm?'

'The snakes around here—are they all poisonous?'

'No, not all,' he answered absently, then his head swivelled towards her with a frown. 'Why, did you see one?'

Bernadette gave him a sickly smile. 'Not in time, I'm afraid.'

He was instantly on his feet, grasping her arms to lower her to the ground.

'Where?'

'My ankle. The right one.'

'Describe the snake.' He'd already found the puncture marks below her rolled-up jeans, and his right hand dived into his pocket for a Swiss Army knife even as he spoke.

'Dark green, small, no more than two feet long, I'd say.'

'Any marks—rings, diamonds, anything like that?'

'No, not that I noticed. Oh!' She cried out as the blade of the knife made two swift incisions in the shape of an X directly over the puncture wounds. 'Sam, you're not actually going to——'

But he was, she discovered as he lowered his head. He sucked hard on the incisions, then spat blood and whatever else he'd extracted on to the ground, repeating the process until Bernadette's ankle hurt more from his ministrations than from the snake bite.

'I thought they only did that in Hollywood Westerns,' she quipped to cover her fear and the discomfort he was causing. 'Couldn't that make you sick?' It was making *her* sick, just watching.

He ignored her nervous babbling. 'Was he in the water?' he asked between sucking and spitting, and Bernadette almost giggled.

'No, on the bank. Do you think you know what kind it was?'

He finally sat back with a grim shake of his head. 'It could be one of a dozen species. Some are venomous, some aren't. We'll just have to wait, and pray this one wasn't.' He reached up to run an agitated hand through his hair. 'I should have brought the medical kit. It's got anti-venom serum and syringes.'

Bernadette laid a hand on his arm. 'It's not your fault,' she said softly. 'I shouldn't have taken off my shoes and socks. And you did warn me to watch out for snakes that first day, remember?

Sam clamped his hand over hers and didn't answer, his mouth a thin, straight line and his eyes dark with concern.

There was no question of continuing on to Lubumbashi, not until Sam decided enough time had elasped to rule out the possibility that the snake had been poisonous. If she didn't develop a fever in the next three or four hours, he said, they'd go on. In the meantime, at least they were near water and a safe distance from Tzongari's camp and the fighting there.

Two hours later Bernadette was definitely feverish, and an hour after that she began to hallucinate. She was unaware of Sam stripping her or carrying her into the pool, his eyes dark with anxiety. Several times during the night and the following day he repeated the ritual, immersing her to the neck to bring down her temperature; and each time it quickly rose again until her skin burned under his hands and he lifted her in his arms to head for the stream once more.

He didn't sleep, and since he'd have had to leave her to find food, neither did he eat. Around midday he thought she felt just a little cooler, but he was afraid it might only be wishful thinking. He watched her constantly, on guard for any more convulsions like the one she'd had during the night, and he prayed. For the first time since he was a child, he prayed—alternately begging and threatening the Almighty, so overwrought that lucidity was beyond him. He knew he had to sleep, get some rest, but he didn't dare doze off just yet. Not until the fever broke and he knew she was over the worst of it. He rose wearily and went to the bank of the stream, kneeling to splash water in his face, keeping his eyes wide open. Slightly refreshed, he sat on the bank, knees bent, and dropped his head into his hands.

Bernadette's eyes came open slowly. Her vision was filled with green, one enormous green blur. It took a few seconds for the shapes of the individual leaves to become distinct, and then she realised that she was lying on her back under towering trees. And that she was stark naked.

What on earth!

She closed her eyes again, trying to think, to remember, but her brain felt like it was covered with a layer of cotton quilt batting. Africa. She was in Africa. She had a fleeting memory of a big old plane lifting off into the sky, and then everything came back in a rush.

Sam. Where was Sam? She tried to sit up, but her body responded sluggishly. Oh, she felt awful, like she was sick or something. Then she remembered. Of course, she'd been bitten by a snake. But Sam had taken care of it, hadn't he? He'd drawn out all the poison. Where *was* he? Why had he gone off and left her alone—and naked, at that—when she was obviously sick as a dog? Her last clear thought was that she would certainly give him a piece of her mind the next time she saw him.

When she next regained consciousness he was sitting cross-legged beside her. She frowned up at him.

'You look like I feel.' She was surprised when her voice came out a hoarse, weak croak.

She actually saw the relief wash through him. His pinched, drawn features relaxed a little, and the haunted look in his eyes moderated to worry as he laid a hand against her cheek.

'I ought to look like hell,' he said, his voice rough. 'God knows that's where I've been the past two days. And you're still burning up.'

'Am I?' Bernadette's eyes dropped, then she forced them open again, mumbling, 'Why am I so sleepy?'

'It's the fever. From the snake bite,' he explained. His fingers gently brushed a strand of damp, lank hair from her face. 'You've had me half out of my mind with worry.'

'I'm sorry,' Bernadette murmured penitently. Then she frowned again, struggling to assimilate what he'd said. 'Am I going to die, Sam?'

His face suddenly tautened again, his eyes burning with a fierce light. 'Don't talk rubbish! Of course you're bloody well not going to die!'

'How can you be sure?' Bernadette whispered. After all, they had no medicine, not even aspirin.

'Because I'm damned well not going to let you!' he retorted furiously.

'But you're scared, I can tell.' Somehow, she was amazingly calm. It must be the fever, she decided; otherwise she'd be scared witless, herself.

'I know you are, because you're mad,' she added

when he glared at her. 'You always get mad when you're afraid.'

Sam gazed down at her in tight-lipped silence for a moment, then muttered: 'You're delirious. Time for another ducking, I think.'

She didn't complain when he scooped her up in his arms, simply because it was what she'd been wanting him to do ever since she opened her eyes. He carried her to the edge of the stream, then glanced down at her. 'Put you arms around my neck and hang on tight. This will be quite a shock.'

And then he plunged into the stream, barely giving her time to follow his instructions. Bernadette gasped as the water hit her fevered skin, her arms tightening around his neck in a stranglehold.

'Oh, Sam, it's like ice!'

Sam shifted his grip to hold her more securely, his hand firm on the underside of her thigh, and Bernadette's stomach contracted sharply. He hesitated briefly, glancing down at her through narrowed eyes, his jaw stern, and then strode through the pool and directly under the waterfall.

'What are you doing!' Bernadette choked, her hands clenching on his shoulders as he withdrew the arm supporting her legs.

'It seems a lot safer than the way I've been doing it,' Sam muttered as he steadied her with a hand at her waist.

'Safer!' she repeated, her teeth chattering like castanets. 'Sam! P-please . . . let me out!'

She was trembling so badly she could hardly stand, goosebumps lifting the fine hairs on her body as she clung to him. She felt him tense, start to withdraw, and she wrapped her arms around his bare chest to hold him. Even dripping wet, his body heat was enough to combat the freezing water cascading over her.

'My mistake,' she heard him say hoarsely. 'This way is definitely not safer. Bernie——'

Both hands went to her waist to force her away a little, and she lifted her face in appeal. She both heard and saw his breath catch as he gazed down at her. And then suddenly Bernadette wasn't cold any more—how could she be, when the raw hunger in his eyes was lighting a fire inside her?

His name whispered past her lips on a sigh of unbearable yearning, and she swayed towards him. And then he was bending to her with a husky groan, his arms pressing her flesh to his in an agony of needing and wanting.

He lifted her, still holding her to him, devouring her mouth with his kiss, and carried her to the bank of the stream, where he laid her gently down. Their mouths kept reaching for one another greedily, pressing heated kisses on faces and necks, shoulders and breasts, while he quickly rid himself of his clothes, never drawing completely out of her grasp.

'Forgive me,' he rasped as he pulled her against his eager body. 'I can't help myself. Oh, darling, I thought you were dying!' His voice shook, then broke at the end as he locked his mouth on hers with a hunger so devastating it nearly had her swooning in his arms.

'Sam!' Bernadette gasped when he broke away to rain kisses over her face. 'You called me darling! Does that mean . . . do you love me?'

'Yes! Forever!' he vowed fiercely. 'Love you and need you. *Now*, Bernie. I need you *now*!'

A shudder racked his powerful frame, echoed by the shiver of pure joy which raced through her. She clasped him to her, one arm around his neck, her fingers buried in his wet hair, the other hand pressed flat on the tensed muscles of his back.

His lovemaking was wild, almost savage, and yet she sensed the way he held back in the beginning, not wanting to hurt her any more than he had to. She rewarded his restraint in the way she met and matched his passion—withholding nothing from him, hurling her body up to meet his, not even trying to stifle the animal sounds which broke from her throat. Her response drove him half out of his mind, and by the time they lay spent and utterly exhausted in one another's arms, they were both too drained to move.

'Bernie,' he murmured after endless minutes, his

mouth moving sensuously against her throat. And then
he lifted his head, and she watched her happiness
disintegrate as a hard, set look came over his face.

'What have I done?' he said heavily. 'Oh, Bernie,
what have I done?'

That had been almost twenty-four hours ago. Since
then he'd barely spoken ten words to her, and he'd been
so coldly distant, denying all her attempts to break
through the barrier he'd erected between them.

Bernadette leaned her head back against the side of
the farm truck they'd hitched a ride in, and closed her
eyes. She felt defeated, her heart a dead thing in her
breast. Or if not dead, wounded beyond healing. She'd
needed tenderness, compassion after they had made
love, and instead he had turned into an aloof stranger.
If he'd shown anger, or guilt—anything—she might
have found the courage and the patience to endure, the
hope to believe that eventually she'd be able to get
through to him. But he deliberately and effectively shut
her out, and in her already weakened state she was
helpless to know how to cope.

She heard the scrape of a match, and then smelled the
pungent aroma of a cheroot, and hopeless tears filled
her closed eyes. Would she ever be able to smell cigar
smoke again in her life without seeing his face?

'Are you asleep?' There was no emotion in the
question, just an impartial curiosity, and she shook her
head listlessly. 'You should be. At the rate we're going
it could take another hour to get there, and God knows
you could use some rest.'

She supposed she should be grateful he was at least
talking to her, but the flat disinterest in his words took
all the joy out of hearing them. She didn't answer; let
him think she'd fallen asleep, what did it matter
any more? What did anything matter, any more?

CHAPTER TWELVE

THE airport terminal was a madhouse as people swarmed through it, all the faces, including Sam's, wearing tense, grim looks. He kept a firm grip on her arm as he bulldozed a path to the ticket counter, and in minutes had her booked on the next flight out.

'You'll go direct to Salisbury. They're boarding now,' he said tersely as he handed her the ticket and boarding pass. 'You'd better hustle.'

Bernadette stood before him in abject misery. She couldn't help thinking that as soon as he saw her off, he would no doubt return to lead Prince Tzongari to the weapons he'd stashed. After that, she didn't dare let herself speculate on what he might be doing.

'Well, I guess this is goodbye.' The stilted words nearly choked her as she formally offered her hand.

Sam's brow furrowed as he hesitated, and then he took it, his grip hard and firm. 'Take care of yourself,' he growled around the stub of his cheroot.

Bernadette nodded, her eyes misting. 'You, too, Colonel.'

And then she had to leave, before she broke down and humiliated them both. She practically ran to the boarding gate, and only after she was through it did she stop and look back.

He was standing where she'd left him, the cheroot clamped between his teeth, his brows nearly touching over his nose, his hands jammed deep in his pockets. Bernadette lifted her hand in a final gesture of farewell, then turned away for the second time. She was halfway up the steps to the plane when she heard him bellow her name. She stopped, blinking to clear her vision as she looked back.

'*Sam*, dammit!' he snarled around the cheroot. He took the few steps necessary to bring him up against the chain link barricade, one hand lifting to the wire mesh.

'If I've told you once, I've told you a dozen times—*Sam*! I'm not any bloody kind of colonel any more!'

He sounded positively furious, and Bernadette's heart leapt from its sickbed with a joyful whoop.

'All right . . . *Sam*, dammit!' she yelled back at him, and saw him stiffen in astonishment, his teeth nearly bisecting the cigar. She began to climb the remaining steps, a smile breaking out as she reached the top and turned.

'By the way . . . Sam,' she called in a clear, strong voice. 'I've been meaning to tell you—*I'm* not really any bloody kind of *nun*!'

She stood poised in the cabin doorway as she watched his reaction. The cheroot—or what was left of it—was flung away and both his hands came up to grip the fence as if he intended to rip a hole in it.

'*What* did you say!'

His tone held stunned incredulity, and something else; something that caused a throaty laugh to erupt from her throat.

'You heard me!' She laughed again, then whirled around and disappeared inside the plane, his vibrant voice ringing in her ears as he shouted after her.

'Why, you little—! You haven't seen the last of me, Bernie, mark my words!'

Three weeks later Bernadette was alone in the school library, tidying the rows of books, when there was a commotion of some sort outside. She finished the shelf she was working on and went to peer out the window, wondering what on earth had caused such a racket. All she could see was the back end of a battered old truck parked at the school's entrance.

'Delivery for Miss Chapman.'

She spun from the window as the familiar growl sent her heart into a panic and made her breath jam in her throat.

He stood in the door, a cheroot clamped in his teeth, cradling a large wooden box against his chest. He was wearing dusty, sweat-stained fatigues and was in dire need of both a bath and a shave, and Bernadette thought she'd never seen a more gorgeous man in her life.

'Sam!'

His eyes narrowed at the husky breathlessness of her voice, and then he came forward to deposit the box on a table. She saw that it was three-quarters filled with apples.

'For me?' she asked softly, her eyes wide. Where on earth had he got them?

'I'm pulling a switch—tempting Eve, instead of the other way around for a change.'

'You didn't need the apples for that,' Bernadette murmured. He didn't answer, just kept staring at her, his grey eyes hooded. She moistened her suddenly dry lips.

'Well ... thank you. It's the nicest present I've had in——'

'I didn't drive nearly five hundred bloody miles just to bring you a bloody damned box of apples,' he grated around the cigar, then snatched it from his mouth and looked around impatiently for a place to stick it. He finally settled for her half empty coffee cup on the desk.

'Then——' Her voice dropped suddenly, becoming unconsciously seductive as she whispered, 'You mean you brought me something else?'

Sam swore under his breath, and then he was advancing on her, the intent in his eyes heating her blood.

'Yes!' he rasped as his lean fingers locked around her wrist. Me!'

He started pulling her behind a bookcase, and Bernadette gave a husky, nervous little laugh.

'Oh! Well that's certainly a——'

'Shut up!' He turned abruptly, yanking her up against him. As their bodies collided his hands came up to capture her face.

'It might not be the most appropriate time and place, but by God, I figured I've earned this!' he muttered, and then his open mouth fastened on hers with a wild, ravenous hunger.

Bernadette moaned as her arms flew around his neck, arching against him, rejoicing in the solid strength of his lean, hard frame. She felt him tremble at her brazen response, and then his hands were slipping through her hair, running down her back with an urgent haste, coming to rest on her softly rounded bottom. His body slid against hers as he stooped to fit her more intimately to him, then he straightened, holding her off the floor.

'Oh, yes, that's much better,' Bernadette sighed as she wriggled against him.

His breath came in shallow gusts as he stared down at her as if he'd never seen her before. 'You—! All this time... all those nights, when we could have been—I ought to strangle you! Or beat you within an inch of your life!'

'I'd much rather you just keep on doing what you're doing now,' Bernadette said in a throaty murmur as her fingers raked through his hair. She felt him stir against her, and her body hummed and throbbed in response.

'Letting me think you were a *nun*!'

'But you know I'm not, now,' she breathed against his neck, her tongue darting out to taste his salty skin.

'You tricked me, *lied* to me, deliberately! Made an utter *fool* of me ... put me through *hell*! And all the time——'

'Shut up and kiss me, Colonel,' Bernadette murmured impatiently, then locked her mouth on his with an insistent hunger that drew a groan from deep in his throat.

'Bernie, Bernie.'

He moaned her name against her lips, and then at her temple, and her closed eyes. It seemed to be all he could say, the only word he knew. She remembered how she'd once been incensed by his lazy, mocking use of that butchered form of Bernadette, and decided she had been a pathetic little idiot. She smiled as he lifted his head to gaze down at her, a heat in his eyes that scorched.

'I love you,' she whispered simply.

'Oh, Bernie!' It came out strangled, almost incomprehensible.

'I do. I love you so much, Sam—so much I ache inside.'

He shook his head helplessly as his arms nearly squeezed the breath out of her. 'Bernie, sweet heaven!'

'I've been waiting all my life for you. The last three weeks have been hell. I've been worried sick that something might happen to you and I'd never have the chance to say it. So I'm saying it now, while I've got the chance. I love you.'

She repeated it over and over while she planted soft, eager kisses on his stubbled jaw and hard-boned face.

'I love you, Sam. I love you, I love you. *God*, how I love you!'

She only stopped when he silenced her with a kiss so passionately intense it made her sag in his arms.

'Where can we go?' he muttered thickly when he could bear to pull away.

'I——' She struggled for breath, trying frantically to think of a place. 'Oh, Sam, I don't know! It's parents' visiting day—there are people everywhere!'

He swore irritably and then scooped her up in his arms and headed for the door.

'Sam!' Bernadette protested as she struggled to tug her skirt down. 'For heaven's sake! What will Mrs Althoff say?'

'Not a damned thing, if she knows what's good for her,' he growled.

Bernadette grinned up at him and looped her arms around his neck. 'Are you carrying me off to ravish me?'

'You bet I am.'

'Oh, goody! Will you have me back in time for tea?'

'Honey, I may not have you back in time for *Christmas*, but I promise you'll get at least one present.'

Bernadette laughed, oblivious to the startled looks on the faces of the people they passed in the hall, as well as Mrs A's indulgent smile as she watched from her office door.

Sam strode purposefully out the front entrance and around to the back of the covered truck, where he unceremoniously dumped her over the tailgate. She landed on a pile of laundry bags, and before she could get over her surprise the door of the cab slammed shut and the truck lurched into motion.

He still drives like a madman, she thought as she wrestled with her clothes and at the same time tried to brace herself, to keep from being thrown against the canvas sides or bounced out the back. She slipped her bra off just as he braked hard and sent her sprawling on her back. She started to wriggle out of her panties, then changed her mind and sank back with a wicked grin.

Seconds later Sam's upper torso appeared above the tailgate. When he saw her, he froze, his hand clenching on the battered, rusty metal.

'Merry Christmas,' Bernadette murmured huskily.

It was glorious, even better than before. She helped him peel off his clothes, her hands for once more sure than his, and then fell back, pulling him down with her and on her. He was tender, yet impatient, alternating incredible gentleness with barbaric demand, and Bernadette gave herself up to the pleasure with joyous abandon, responsive to every nuance of his quicksilver moods. They spoke no words; none were needed. They were in perfect accord, their minds and bodies and souls fusing and melding and their hearts thundering in unison. Sam strained to fill her completely, giving her everything and receiving everything in return, until there was nothing left to give and they lay in a satiated stupor, waiting for the world to right itself.

'Incredible,' Sam breathed as he shifted her to rest on his chest.

Bernadette nestled closer with a smile. 'Yes, wasn't it?'

'I meant you,' he drawled, kissing the top of her head.

'Oh.' She smiled again. 'But we are awfully good together—aren't we?'

His 'Oh, God!' was a ragged but fervent sigh. He was silent for a moment, then muttered in a gruff voice, 'I'm old enough to be your father.'

'Yes, I suppose you are,' she agreed, tenderly amused by this sudden display of anxiety. Or was it self-doubt?

'All the odds are against us. We have virtually nothing in common,' he went on glumly.

Bernadette let her hand wander down his side until it came to rest on his hip. 'We will have. Especially after the first baby comes.'

'What next?' He sounded both exasperated and horrified. 'Now she's prattling on about *babies*! Bernie, I'm trying to make you see how impossible——'

'You don't want babies?' She tilted her head to look up at him, disappointment in her voice and her eyes. 'You don't like children, is that it? Or maybe you just don't want to have any with me?'

Doubt battled awestruck wonder for supremacy as Sam gazed down at her earnest face. And then he suddenly pulled her up, feeling her smooth, warm flesh slide over his, and kissed her hard on the mouth.

'How about three, to start with,' he said in a voice roughened by emotion.

Bernadette smiled into his eyes. 'Let's make it four—two of each. And they'll all be named Forrester,' she added sternly.

Sam's mouth quirked at the way her lips compressed in determination. 'Is that a proposal of marriage?' he drawled.

'Well, I thought *one* of us should bring it up!'

His eyes glinted and he pursed his lips to keep them from stretching into a moronic grin.

'Okay, I'll marry you,' he conceded lazily, and watched her violet eyes flash before she lowered her lashes to shield them from him. Apparently she decided not to let him bait her, because she only muttered, 'Thank goodness that's settled.' She hesitated, then asked, her voice low, 'Will you be going back to help Prince Tzongari, now?'

'No,' Sam assured her with a tender smile. 'If I'm going to have this enormous family to support, I'd better start behaving more responsibly,' he added in a mocking drawl.

Bernadette gazed at him steadily. 'Will you mind very much? I mean, giving up all the adventure, the excitement?'

Sam's eyes were suddenly full of devilment. 'The adventure associated with sitting in on day-long meetings, you mean? The excitement of negotiating rush hour traffic in Nairobi, or Dar es Salaam?'

Bernadette's eyes narrowed and she stared at him a

moment before demanding suspiciously, 'What exactly do you *do*, when you're not helping old buddies try to set up their own country?'

'What's the matter, afraid I won't be able to support you and the kiddos?' he teased with a straight face.

'And what was that about meetings, and rush hour traffic? Dar what? Stop grinning like a brainless idiot and answer me, Sam Forrester!'

He easily foiled her attempt to push away from him, lifting his head to plant a light kiss on the end of her nose.

'Just waiting for the chance to get a word in, darling,' he said in amusement. Then he suddenly sobered. 'Would it disappoint you very much to discover I'm not the romantic soldier of fortune you obviously took me for?'

Bernadette hesitated, still suspicious, then murmured, 'Claude told me you occasionally help out old friends, and you *were* delivering guns and ammunition to Prince Tzongari.'

' "Delivering" being the key word,' Sam stressed. 'I never had any intention of taking part in his little rebellion, nor did he expect me to.'

By now Bernadette was thoroughly confused, and it showed. 'Well then, if you're not some kind of glorified mercenary, what *are* you, for heaven's sake!' she demanded in exasperation.

Sam sighed, his mouth rueful. 'Nothing more than a private businessman, I'm afraid,' he muttered wryly. 'I bring people together—mainly reps from multinational corporations looking for a base in Africa, and government officials trying to attract new businesses. When I retired from the army, I knew I wanted to stay in this part of the world, and it occurred to me that there was a need for that kind of service, so . . .' He let a shrug finish the explanation. 'I have a legitimate reason to indulge my passion for travel, I get to visit old friends in the course of my work, and now and then do a favour for one. I'm my own boss. If I feel like taking a week or two off to hang around the bars of Mombasa and play poker, that's what I do. You can meet some of the most interesting characters in those seedy water-fronts bars,' he added blandly.

Bernadette stared at him expressionlessly, letting the seconds stretch out until he began to look a little harried, just a bit anxious.

'So,' she finally murmured, her tone unrevealing. She made him wait another minute or so, then added drily, 'My father will absolutely love you. It's really ironic. *I* came to Africa looking for adventure, excitement—to get away from the world I grew up in, where I was surrounded by talk of business deals and legal disputes.' She shook her head with a disgruntled frown.

Sam's brows pulled together as he gazed at her, his eyes solemn. 'You are disappointed,' he muttered heavily.

Bernadette shrugged, not quite ready to let him off the hook. 'I imagine I'll get over it.' Her hand glided over his stomach and up his chest, her touch light yet erotic as a mischievous twinkle appeared in her eyes. 'We'll just have to make our own excitement, Colonel. What do you think—can a surly jungle commando and a bogus nun find true happiness together, forever, when all the odds are against them?'

Sam's eyes lit from within, his features relaxing as he ran a hand up her back, his palm hard against her nape. He held her gaze, his lean, strong fingers caressing her scalp slowly, making her weak with longing, and then a wicked grin claimed his mouth as he pulled her down to him.

'There's no doubt in my mind,' he murmured huskily against her parted lips. And then he caught her to him and proceeded to show *her* just what *he* meant by 'forever'.

Coming Next Month

895 STORM Vanessa Grant
After being stranded by a fierce storm in the Queen Charlotte Islands a reporter doubts herself, the hard-hitting pilot she desires and her commitment to a childhood sweetheart.

896 LOSER TAKE ALL Rosemary Hammond
A wealthy American doesn't exactly win his new bride in a poker game. But it amounts to the same thing, because it's marriage for them—win or lose!

897 THE HARD MAN Penny Jordan
Desire for a virtual stranger reminds a young widow and mother she is still a woman capable of love, capable of repeating the mistake she made ten years ago.

898 EXPLOSIVE MEETING Charlotte Lamb
A lab technician's boss resents his employee's impassioned plea on behalf of a brilliant scientist who keeps blowing up the lab. And he misinterprets her persistence—in more ways than one!

899 AN ALL-CONSUMING PASSION Anne Mather
When her father's right-hand man comes to the Caribbean to escort the boss's daughter back to London, she tries to make him forget his responsibilities—never thinking she is playing with fire.

900 LEAVING HOME Leigh Michaels
A young woman never dreams her guardian's decision to remain single had anything to do with her, until he proposes marriage—to pull her out of yet another scrape.

901 SUNSTROKE Elizabeth Oldfield
Can a widow reconcile receiving twenty thousand pounds to pay off her late husband's creditors with leaving the man she loves—even though he's been groomed to marry someone else?

902 DANGEROUS MOONLIGHT Kay Thorpe
It is possible that the Greek hotel owner a vacationer encounters isn't the same man who ruined her sister's marriage. But can she risk asking him outright, when the truth could break her heart?

Available in July wherever paperback books are sold, or through Harlequin Reader Service.

In the U.S.
901 Fuhrmann Blvd.
P.O. Box 1397
Buffalo, N.Y. 14240-1397

In Canada
P.O. Box 2800, Postal Station A
5170 Yonge Street
Willowdale, Ontario M2N 6J3